This month, in **TEXAS MILLIONAIRE**
by Dixie Browning, meet oil baron
Henry "Hank" Langley, owner of the prestigious
Texas Cattleman's Club. Nothing fazes Hank, not
even the dangerous secret mission he's about to
undertake, until…homemaker-at-heart
Callie Riley—a fresh-faced, understated,
younger beauty—walks into his life!

**SILHOUETTE DESIRE
IS PROUD TO PRESENT THE**

**Five wealthy Texas bachelors—all members
of the state's most exclusive club—set out on a
mission to rescue a princess…and find true love.**

* * *

**And don't miss CINDERELLA'S TYCOON
by Caroline Cross, next month's installment
of the *Texas Cattleman's Club*, available in
Silhouette Desire!**

Dear Reader,

Silhouette Desire matches August's steamy heat with six new powerful, passionate and provocative romances.

Popular Elizabeth Bevarly offers *That Boss of Mine* as August's MAN OF THE MONTH. In this irresistible romantic comedy, a CEO falls for his less-than-perfect secretary.

And Silhouette Desire proudly presents a compelling new series, TEXAS CATTLEMAN'S CLUB. The members of this exclusive club are some of the Lone Star State's sexiest, most powerful men, who go on a mission to rescue a princess and find true love! Bestselling author Dixie Browning launches the series with *Texas Millionaire*, in which a fresh-faced country beauty is wooed by an older man.

Cait London's miniseries THE BLAYLOCKS continues with *Rio: Man of Destiny*, in which the hero's love leads the heroine to the truth of her family secrets. The BACHELOR BATTALION miniseries by Maureen Child marches on with *Mom in Waiting*. An amnesiac woman must rediscover her husband in *Lost and Found Bride* by Modean Moon. And Barbara McCauley's SECRETS! miniseries offers another scandalous tale with *Secret Baby Santos*.

August also marks the debut of Silhouette's original continuity THE FORTUNES OF TEXAS with Maggie Shayne's *Million Dollar Marriage*, available now at your local retail outlet.

So indulge yourself this month with some poolside reading— the first of THE FORTUNES OF TEXAS, and all six Silhouette Desire titles!

Enjoy!

Joan Marlow Golan
Senior Editor

Please address questions and book requests to:
Silhouette Reader Service
U.S.: 3010 Walden Ave., P.O. Box 1325, Buffalo, NY 14269
Canadian: P.O. Box 609, Fort Erie, Ont. L2A 5X3

TEXAS
MILLIONAIRE
DIXIE BROWNING

SILHOUETTE Desire

TM

Published by Silhouette Books

America's Publisher of Contemporary Romance

For fellow Cattleman's Club members
Caroline Cross, Peggy Moreland, Metsy Hingle
and Cindy Gerard. Ladies,
I'll ride the range with you anytime! Move 'em out!

Special thanks and acknowledgment are given to
Dixie Browning for her contribution to the
Texas Cattleman's Club miniseries.

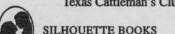 SILHOUETTE BOOKS

ISBN 0-373-76232-1

TEXAS MILLIONAIRE

Copyright © 1999 by Harlequin Books S.A.

Visit us at www.romance.net

Printed in U.S.A.

Books by Dixie Browning

DIXIE BROWNING

celebrates her sixty-fifth book for Silhouette with the publication of *Texas Millionaire*. She has also written a number of historical romances with her sister under the name Bronwyn Williams. A charter member of Romance Writers of America, and a member of Novelists, Inc., Dixie has won numerous awards for her work. She divides her time between Winston-Salem and the Outer Banks of North Carolina.

"What's Happening in Royal?"

NEWS FLASH, August 1999—The town of Royal, TX, is all abuzz as to which society beauty Hank Langley, the owner of the prestigious Texas Cattleman's Club, will take to the annual Cattleman's Ball. Will it be socialite Pansy Ann Estrich? Or glamour girl Bianca Mullins? And will his date become the future *Mrs.* Langley?

And speaking of women in the wealthy Mr. Langley's life, who *is* Callie Riley, his new young secretary, who's just appeared on the scene?

Rumors are also running rampant about some late-night meetings at the Texas Cattleman's Club. What could be brewing among the members? Stay tuned....

One

Boot heels propped on the polished walnut windowsill, Hank Langley watched a small jet plane cross his field of vision with deceptive slowness. Absently he tugged up his pants leg and massaged the expanse of scarred, muscular flesh between the top of his custom-made boot and the bottom of his custom-tailored jeans.

He ached. Damn front coming through. If it would bring rain, it would be worth the ache, but it hadn't rained enough to lay the dust all year. August was August. West Texas was West Texas.

And hot was hot.

Miss Manie rapped once on his door and entered. She was scrupulous about affording him a five-second warning, in case he was up to God knows what behind closed doors.

"You're hurting again, aren't you?"

"No, ma'am."

"Don't you tell me one of your teewydies, young man,

you were out until all hours, giving that limb of yours a fit, weren't you?''

Teewydie was Romania Riley's euphemism for a polite lie. Evidently it was a Carolina thing. Hank had never heard anyone from Texas use the term. ''You know where I was. You know who I was with. If you want a blow-by-blow account, grab yourself a tall, cold beer and take a seat.''

He'd been out with Pansy Ann Estrich, as Manie damned well knew. Wining and dining her, trying to work himself up to committing to something he was nowhere ready to commit to, for no better reason than it was time—it was past time—and the choice had narrowed down to two women. Pansy and Bianca Mullins. Both women were in their middle thirties. Both knew the score. Neither was looking for more in a relationship than he was capable of offering. Personally he thought it was a pretty good deal. Sex, of course. Security, insured by a prenuptial agreement that was fair to both parties. Companionship, and at least one, preferably two, offspring. Preferably male.

''Well?'' Miss Manie's wattles quivered as she waited for enlightenment.

''Well?'' Hank tossed back at her.

''Don't get smart with me, Henry Langley. I knew you back when you couldn't step out the front door without running head-on into trouble.'' She glared at him through the upper half of her bifocals, then glanced down at her notes. ''Speaking of trouble, Miss Pansy was on the phone first thing this morning about the Cattleman's Ball. You didn't ask her last night, did you?''

''Ask her which, to the ball or to marry me?''

She gave him a look she'd perfected before he'd ever been born. Manie was going to be a problem, no matter which woman he married. ''The answer to both questions,'' he said dryly, ''is not yet.''

He had to be the only six-foot-two, ex-special services millionaire in Texas who allowed himself to be pushed around by ninety-odd pounds of outspoken spinster.

"I wouldn't jump into anything too fast, if I were you. There's plenty of time. Oh, and while I've got you, Preacher Weldon wants to know about the belfry, and they were short of red roses at the florist, so I sent Bianca pink ones, instead. If you ask me, she was hoping for something a lot more substantial than a bunch of flowers."

Hank refrained from sighing. He'd gone out with Bianca Mullins three times last week, exploring the possibility of spending the rest of his life with a woman who had the body of a centerfold and the brain of a high school dropout.

At least she had a sense of humor. Pansy didn't.

He flexed his shoulders in an effort to relieve the tension, stroked his pants leg down to cover his scarred flesh and swung his feet down off the windowsill. Miss Manie had lectured him more than a few times about his habit of plopping his feet on the furniture, but dammit, it was his furniture, his office—damned near his town.

And he ached. His left leg still carried a few pieces of scrap metal from the crash that ended his military career. It caused some problems with airport security, but otherwise, it was no big deal unless there was a sudden drop in barometric pressure. According to the team of surgeons who had worked him over, retrieving every last fragment would have caused more damage than it was worth.

That was a matter of opinion, but he willingly accepted responsibility for the occasional ache. He'd been the one to run off and join the Air Force against his parents' wishes. Back in those days he'd been into rebellion, big time.

"Yes, ma'am," he said meekly. "I'll deal with Pansy and Bianca, you can tell the reverend to call in his carpenters, and pink ones are fine, unless you know something about the language of flowers that's going to land me in trouble.''

''Hmmph. Nobody these days pays any attention to that kind of thing. Leastwise, none of those women of yours.''

''You make it sound like I'm supporting a harem.''

Saved by the bell. Hank had two cell phones and a private line, but most calls were routed through Miss Manie's desk. On the second ring, Manie said, ''I'd better get that, it's probably the kitchen about those temporaries we're fixing to hire for the ball, but remind me to tell you about my great-niece when you have a minute.''

Her great-niece? What, had the kid graduated from high school or something? He'd send her the usual. There was always somebody on his staff with a kid graduating from somewhere. Manie could handle it. She always handled the personal side of his life. Not that her relatives were his personal business. He hadn't even known, except in the vaguest terms, that she had any relatives left back in North Carolina. Considering how long she'd been a part of his life, he knew surprisingly little about the woman who served as conscience, security guard, surrogate mother and outspoken personal assistant, other than the fact that her only brother had died a year or so ago.

One more testimony to what a self-centered bastard he was.

The streak of dirty tan sky that showed between the linen drapes grew paler as the wind picked up, blowing clouds of sand and salt from the dry bed of Salt Lake. ''Rain, dammit,'' Hank grumbled. ''Go ahead, cut loose. I dare you.''

He was limping. He almost never limped. Hated any sign of weakness, in fact. But then, when a man was facing middle age, it was only natural that he began to show a few signs of wear and tear.

Pity he had so damned little else to show for his years, but he was working on it. He'd given himself until his rapidly approaching fortieth birthday to settle the course of his future.

He took Pansy Estrich to dinner again that night, because she'd waited until Miss Manie had left for the day and poked her head into his private office, offering him one of her winsome smiles. "Hank, can we talk?"

He'd been looking forward to a long, hot soak in the king-size bathtub he'd had installed a few years ago, followed by a double order of his chef's garlic-grilled gulf shrimp, a fine cigar, a stiff drink and good night's sleep.

Fat chance. Until he came to a decision, talking to either woman was risky business. He was still hovering on the brink of making a decision, and dammit, he refused to be shoved. But he said, "Give me time to wind up some business, and we'll have dinner. Pick you up in an hour?"

"Why don't I just browse the shops and then come back?"

"Fine. Meet you downstairs in one hour."

Hank lived above the sprawling, exclusive gentlemen's club his grandfather, Henry "Tex" Langley, had established nearly ninety years ago. He maintained an office there, with an anteroom office for Manie, the only woman with free access into his private domain. For a single businessman it was an ideal setup, but if he chose to marry, he was going to have to make some changes. Wives were territorial. Neither of the two finalists liked Manie, and the feeling was entirely mutual.

Besides, the club was no place to raise a family. Despite the ladies' parlor his father had set aside, it was still primarily a male domain, and Hank intended to enjoy it until the bitter end.

"Or I could wait for you up here," Pansy said hopefully.

He nearly blurted, Good God, are you still here? "Thanks, but old Tex would roll over in his grave." Hank knew better than to set any precedents. Give a woman an inch and the rest was history.

For the next forty-five minutes he played phone tag with club member Greg Hunt, who'd left a cryptic message earlier, talked to his broker, to the head of his accounting firm and to the chief designer at the avionics firm that built his new Avenger with a suggestion for making the flight deck more pilot-friendly.

Through it all, the feeling of being in the crosshairs persisted. Being a matrimonial target was nothing new to a bachelor pushing forty who happened to be the sole owner of the exclusive Texas Cattleman's Club as well as the state's biggest oil baron, according to a prominent financial journalist.

All the same, there were days when he felt like nothing so much as a side of fresh beef thrown into a pool filled with hungry sharks.

Oil baron. He hated the sound of it, but it had been applied to the men of his family for three generations. It had started out way back in the early part of the century when Langley One had blown in, followed within the week by three more, all flowing at better than ninety barrels per day. His father, Henry, Jr., had expanded the family business by leasing drilling rights all across the south, including the Gulf of Mexico. Some were still operative, but only about ten percent of the Langley wealth was tied up in oil at the moment. Most of Hank's investments were in technology, Texas having already moved ahead of Silicon Valley in the computer field.

But wealth was wealth and women were women, and regardless of his decision that it was time to marry if he ever intended to, Hank had no intention of going meekly to the highest bidder.

At Claire's, the town's finest French restaurant, Hank ordered his usual rare sirloin with a side of lobster, hold the fancy sauces. Pansy, wearing a casual outfit the color of dry sand that matched her hair perfectly, spent fifteen minutes poring over the menu, then ordered her usual Bloody Mary, snails in plain butter, salad with extra dressing, fresh croissants and diet soda.

The long-suffering waiter nodded, and Hank gave him a look of silent commiseration.

Pansy wanted to talk about the club's annual ball. "You didn't invite Bianca, did you? She said you hadn't."

"I've been too busy worrying with the business end to think about the personal end." It was no less than the truth. He'd had a steady stream of charities in and out of his office for the past couple of weeks, eager to hop aboard before the train left the station. Fund-raising was the biggest growth industry in town, and the club's annual ball was *the* charity event of the year, the proceeds being divided among a varying, carefully selected list of local charities.

On the personal side, at last year's event one of Bianca's friends had announced her engagement. The year before, Pansy's younger sister had chosen that particular arena for the same announcement. It was becoming *the* place to announce plans of a matrimonial nature. Hank couldn't get rid of the feeling that the sharks were moving in for the kill.

Pansy waited for the waiter to open her napkin with a fine French flourish and spread it over her lap before launching onto a fresh topic. "Hanky, don't you think it's time to have that old place redecorated? I mean, all that heavy paneling and those ugly old animal heads. It's depressing. Nobody has animal heads these days."

Hanky? "Mounted trophies are traditional."

"Oh, poo on tradition, what you need is something light and cheerful. I could give you a few suggestions," she added coyly.

"I'm sure you could. Look, Pansy, I appreciate it, but the members—"

"They'd love it. You can't tell me anyone wants a herd of gloomy old moose heads glaring down at them all the time. Didn't you ever hear of animal rights? Give the poor things a decent burial."

"What did you have in mind, mounted teddy bears? Or maybe some dried-flower wreaths?"

"Oh, God, you're in one of your moods again, I can tell."

One of his moods? Was he really that bad? He'd thought he was being pretty damn reasonable for a man who was starting to think seriously about marriage for the first time in his life.

The second time, actually, but his first marriage didn't count. If he'd had a functioning brain back then, it had been below the belt.

All the same, Pansy was getting a little too territorial. When anyone, man or woman, moved in on him too fast, old military habits took over and he threw up a barricade.

Or in this case, a red herring. "Speaking of decorating, I've been considering doing something to the Pine Valley house, maybe putting it on the market." It had been his father's house, bought for his fourth wife only two years before they'd both been killed in an avalanche on a skiing trip. Hank had inherited it, along with everything else. He'd hung onto it, not for sentimental reasons, because his father had lived there, but because good real estate was a sound investment.

Pansy pounced like a hound on a ham bone. "Why don't

we run out there after we leave here and look it over? I know this perfectly marvelous decorator in Odessa—Mama had him last spring.''

Pansy's mama had had half the men in Texas. That was no recommendation.

''Uh…I've got to fly up to Midland tonight—'' He invented a business trip on the spur of the moment. ''Maybe when I get back…'' He checked his watch, and then checked it a few more times when she was slow in taking the hint. There was something about that avid look on her face that made him distinctly uneasy as he led her outside the restaurant and signaled for his car to be brought around.

Go ahead, pop the question. What are you waiting for, violins?

Hank told himself he was waiting for his gut to settle down. Even without all the fancy sauces, French food was too rich for his blood, but Pansy loved the place.

He drove her home, as she'd sent her own car home earlier, and walked her to the door. Declining her invitation for a nightcap and whatever else she had in mind, he left her on her doorstep, but not before she kissed him goodnight. Latched on to him like moss on a wet rock and let him have both barrels.

Hell, he was only human. He kissed her back, tasting buttery lipstick, inhaling her overpowering perfume, wishing he felt a spark of interest. Objectively speaking, she was a gorgeous piece of work, and it had been a long dry spell, seeing as how he was inclined to be particular where his sex life was concerned.

And besides, if he was going to marry the woman…

It wasn't enough. He wanted more. Didn't know exactly what it was he was holding out for, but he suspected that Pansy Ann Estrich didn't even come close. So he managed to escape unmolested, then asked himself on the way home if he was being a damned fool to turn down what she was offering, with or without a commitment.

Nah…he wasn't. He was finally facing up to the depressing fact that unless he married and had children of his own, Henry Harrison Langley, III, was a dead end, the last of three generations of spectacularly successful men. The trouble was, he was increasingly certain that Pansy wasn't the answer. For one thing, she didn't like children. For another, she lacked even a vestigial sense of humor.

And then there was the inescapable fact that odds were against any man of his age, and with his family history, making a successful marriage. His grandfather had been widowed twice and divorced once, back in the days when divorce was tantamount to disgrace. His father had run through three more wives after Hank's mother had died giving birth to a stillborn daughter.

Aside from all that—or maybe because of it—he was pretty much of a loner. At the age of seventeen he'd eloped with a fifteen-year-old cheerleader who'd lied about her age. Hank's idea of marriage had been nonstop sex. Tammy's had been nonstop shopping. Major incompatibility. His father had paid her off and had the marriage annulled, which had broken Hank's heart, but opened his eyes.

Inherited wealth had left him with a bitter taste in his mouth, despite the fact that he had managed to triple his inheritance by careful management and shrewd investments. He had a low tolerance for sycophants which, over the years had led to a growing sense of isolation. From youthful recklessness that had carried him through a few high-risk military actions, he'd gradually slipped into a dull sense of reserve that occasionally bordered on the paranoid. He put it down to being who he was: the richest kid in town, who'd done little to prove his own manhood.

Not that he hadn't tried. But ever since his youthful fit of rebellion, his lawyers, both corporate and personal, tended to get antsy if he went out with the same woman more than three times in a row. Pansy and Bianca checked out because they were in his income bracket, give or take a few sets of zeros.

As for Miss Manie, she turned into a fire-breathing dragon whenever she thought he was about to be trapped by one of the women she called scheming hussies and shameless gold diggers. And while he depended on her judgment on most things, the truth was, he was getting pretty damned tired of playing dodge-the-wedding-ring, and the only way he could figure to end the game was to pick out the best of the lot and do the deed.

The red light on his message machine was blinking rapidly when he let himself back into his rooms over the club. Knowing he wouldn't be able to sleep unless he cleared the decks, he switched on the playback. Greg's voice erupted into the quiet room.

"Greg here. Listen, Hank, I think I've got a situation brewing and I'm going to need your help. Probably Forrest and Sterling, too, before it's over. I won't lay it out over the phone, but I need to see you as soon as you can spare some time. It's urgent."

A situation? What the hell was that all about? Methodically, Hank unbuttoned his shirt, eased it off his shoulders, stretched his arms over his head and yawned. God knows, he could do with a distraction. This business of getting himself engaged was the pits.

Romania Riley eased her bunions into a basin of hot Epsom salts, breathed out a sigh and took a swig of her homemade blackberry wine. She'd learned to make it at the age of fourteen, when a jar of improperly sealed, home-canned blackberries had fermented and blown the lid off, spattering everything in the kitchen, Manie included.

For months she'd been fretting over what to do about all the women who were making nuisances of themselves over her boy. Not a single one of them wanted him for the kind, sensitive man he was. All they were interested in was the wealth and position he represented. As if money was the answer to life's problems.

Money hadn't made Hank's father a happy man. As for that old goat, Tex Langley, he'd been the worst scalawag that ever walked on two legs, not that you'd ever hear a word of criticism from the folks of Royal, Texas. He might've fooled most of 'em into thinking he was some kind of saint, but Manie had known the man behind the legend.

She'd been eight and a half years old when her mama had run off and her father, Alaska Riley, had picked up and moved to Louisiana, following the oil company that had been drilling off the coast of North Carolina. They'd lived there for a few months, camping out like gypsies, just the two of them and Pa's old dog, Dog. Dog ran off one night in a thunderstorm. He never did come back, and it broke her father's heart because Dog was family. He'd been even older than Manie at the time.

Manie didn't know how old she'd been before she understood about her father's drinking. She'd always been aware that his moods swung from high good humor to the mean miseries. Following the miseries he'd lay out for a few days, sick as a dog, and then he'd swear off drinking. Manie always got her hopes up, but it never lasted long.

From Louisiana they migrated to Texas. Pa swore off the bottle for nearly six months, and they moved into a two-room house and Manie got to go to school. For a little while, everything was nice as pie. But then, her father fell into bad company. Before long he'd gone back to his old ways. Manie fussed at him because she was scared, but fussing only shoved him into the mean miseries.

There came a time when he took real drunk two days before payday, and Manie without so much as a bean or a biscuit in the house. She couldn't even scrape up ten cents for a loaf of bread, so she hitched a ride into town in a feed truck—back in those days, Royal had been nothing at all like it was now.

Everybody knew where old Tex lived. The man owned practically all of West Texas. She'd hopped off the back of the truck, marched right up the front walk, banged on the door of the Langley mansion, and when the house-keeper had opened the door, she'd demanded the money owed her father for three days' work.

The housekeeper had tried to shoo her away, but Manie refused to budge. Pa would skin her alive if he ever found out what she'd done, but she was desperate and hungry, and she couldn't think of anywhere else to turn.

"You go 'round to the back door, I'll see if Mist' Tex's home."

Manie went. Back door, front door—what difference did it make as long as she got what she came for?

Only she hadn't. The housekeeper had come back and told her that Mr. Tex said to go by the field office Monday morning, and then the woman had slammed the door in her face.

She'd felt like throwing a flower pot through the window, but they'd only sic the dog or call the law, and Pa would find out and get really, really mad.

But she couldn't wait, she was too hungry. She didn't want a check from the field office, either, she wanted real cash money that she could take to the grocery store and buy food before her father got his hands on it and spent it all on whiskey.

So she banged on the door again, reminding herself that she was a Riley, and Rileys were Good People. She could still remember hearing her father say so, back before her mama had picked up and left. In Pa's case, the stock might have run to seed, but Manie knew better than to act like trash. She might be hungry, but she had her pride.

Her knocks went unanswered, and she was too short to reach the big brass knocker. Finally, blinded by tears of sheer frustration, ten-year-old Manie had slammed out the front gate and run head-on into young Henry, who had heard her out, tears, sobs, runny nose and all. Then he'd kindly explained that her father couldn't work out at the field any more because he was too unreliable, and on a drilling rig, that could be dangerous, but that he'd see that she got any back pay coming to him.

Then he'd taken her home to his wife—his first wife—who had given her a glass of buttermilk and offered her a job after school and on weekends helping out in the kitchen.

Mercy, had it really been almost sixty years since then? It had been a wild ride, keeping up with the Langleys, but she wouldn't trade a speck of it for any amount of money. Child to woman, she'd been there through good times and bad, first when old Tex died, then when her father had passed away with the liver trouble, and a year later when Hank was born and a few years after that when Mr. Henry lost his wife and his newborn daughter.

She had watched young Hank grow up, loved him as if he were her own, and done her best to look after him when his father had taken up with one woman after another and gone chasing off to all those fancy places in Europe.

She'd done a fair job of raising the boy, too, if she did

say so herself. She knew his shortcomings and his long-comings and would be the first to admit he had his share of both.

But right now, he was going through another dangerous stage, and it was up to her to see him through it. Temptation was a hard thing to resist when it came all dolled up in tight dresses and blue eye shadow, reeking of fancy perfume and using language no lady ever used in front of a gentleman. That kind of temptation spelled trouble, sure as the world.

But Manie had a plan.

Two

Early on a Saturday morning, shoulders squared, head held high, Callie locked the front door, took one last walk around the house to be sure she'd remembered to close all the windows and fill all the feeders and headed for Texas.

"Grace, I'm on my way. Feed my birds about Wednesday, will you?" she called to her neighbor at the foot of the road.

"I'll check every couple of days. See you in a week or so. Drive safe, have a good time, don't do anything I wouldn't do."

Callie promised, her mind already miles ahead. This was a mission, not a vacation. Never given to impulsive acts, she had thought it through carefully, made her lists, pro and con, and checked one against the other. And now here she was, finally on her way.

By Tuesday, second thoughts were rapidly piling up. Back home in North Carolina, it had all sounded so logical.

Now that she was actually in Texas, she was beginning to wonder if she shouldn't have talked her plan over with Aunt Manie first instead of springing it on her out of the blue.

Quit fretting, Caledonia, it's too late now. You've done all that work on the house and shut off the mail and paper delivery. You buttered your bread, now lie in it.

She was tired, that's all it was. Besides, everything out west was so blessed big. This was the first time she'd ever even crossed to the other side of the Blue Ridge mountains. What in the world had she been thinking?

Back when the idea had first come to her, it seemed like the most logical thing in the world. She'd never even met Great-Aunt Manie until Grandpop Riley's funeral last September, but the two of them had hit it off right away. Aunt Manie was so much like Grandpop, which was perfectly logical. They'd been brother and sister, after all. They shared the same common sense approach to life, the same dry sense of humor. They even looked alike, both being spare of frame and stern of face until you caught the twinkling eyes and the little twitch at the corner of the mouth.

And besides, Aunt Manie used to live in Grandpop's house. It was Callie's now. Nobody else wanted it, at least not to live in. Her father, who had grown up there, called it an old relic, which it was, which was why Grandpop had left it to Callie and not his own son.

It had taken practically all her savings, but she'd fixed the old place up so that Aunt Manie wouldn't give it that sad-eyed look, the way she had after the funeral. A new roof, at least on the south side, where the sun baked the shingles so that they curled up and leaked. A fresh coat of paint in a lovely shade of gray, with contrasting trim. Next she was going to tackle the plumbing and wiring, but first she'd have to find another job and build up her savings again.

But the yard was in fine shape. Surrounded by rhododendrons and weeping cherry trees, flame azalea and the day lilies that Grandpop had called backhouse lilies, it sat plank in the middle of seven acres of woodland a few miles from Brooks Cross Roads. For someone who preferred life in the slow lane, it was ideal.

And Callie was definitely slow-lane material. Driving to Yadkinville five days a week to work was fast enough for her. And at Aunt Manie's age, she was going to fit right in.

Callie's father, Bainbridge, had expected her to sell out as soon as the will had been probated. Ever since he'd given up his position with the insurance company and gone to being a full-time potter and part-time fiddler, he'd been looking for ways to make money. Unlike Callie, he hadn't inherited his father's philosophy of work hard, live cheap and lay by for a rainy day.

He should have thought of that before he'd quit. Her mother was just as bad, but then, Sally Cutler was only a Riley by marriage. Riley tradition didn't mean doodley-squat to her, never had. After working her way up to assistant manager at Big Joe Arther's Motors and playing the organ at the Brushy Creek Church for as long as Callie could remember, Sally had hit menopause. She'd dealt with it by bleaching her hair, eating a lot of soybeans and playing keyboard with a homegrown country rock band who called themselves The Rockin' Possum.

For the past few years Bain and Sally had taken in every fiddler's convention and craft show between Galax and Nashville, leaving Callie and Grandpop to take care of each other. Which suited Callie just fine. She'd had her job, and Grandpop had had his garden.

But then last fall Grandpop had passed over. Died in his sleep, peaceful as a dove. And Callie had finally met his sister Romania, and one thing led to another, and now here she was in Texas, of all places.

Manie had told her back when she'd come east to the funeral that her own roots were in Texas, but Callie hadn't believed it, not for a minute. Her leaves and branches might be in Texas, but Manie's roots were back in the thick red clay of Yadkin County, North Carolina.

Callie hadn't mentioned it at the time, but the plan had already started to simmer in her mind when they'd driven around to see all the new development and the old familiar places. Callie was a good planner. So far as she knew, she was the only truly reliable member of her immediate family, because even Grandpop had run off and joined the Merchant Marine when he was barely old enough to shave.

As for Aunt Manie, it was too soon to tell. If she needed looking after, then Callie was the one to do it. If, on the other hand, she was simply looking for a place to retire, why then, what better place than the home where she'd once lived as a girl? The plain truth was, Callie was lonesome in that big old house. And family was important. Now that Grandpop was gone, and her parents didn't need her—not yet, at least—she was free to look after whichever family member needed her most.

It was the perfect answer for both of them. Once Manie was back in Yadkin County, where Rileys had lived since they'd crossed the Yadkin River on a ferryboat, driving a mule-drawn cart, she'd forget all about the Langleys.

Langleys. To hear her talk, you'd think they were second cousins to God, or something. In the week her aunt had been there, Callie had heard more than enough about their wonderful oil wells, their beautiful mansion and their fancy, exclusive, rich-man's club. At the age of sixty-nine, ac-

cording to Manie—seventy-two, according to Grandpop—
poor Aunt Manie was still slaving away for the last of her
precious Langleys. She'd described him as sweet, sensitive
and vulnerable, with women trying to marry him for his
money.

There was nothing sweet, sensitive, or even decent about
a man who would allow a woman to work years beyond
retirement age when she had a perfectly good home to go
back to and a niece willing and able to look after her.

Besides, he sounded like a wimp. While the term sensitive might apply to old Doc Teeter, the man Callie had
worked for ever since she was sixteen years old, she
couldn't see it applying to a rich, middle-aged bachelor.
The man was obviously spoiled rotten. Probably one of
those playboys who had their picture taken for *People* magazine with models and actresses draped all over him.

Well, Callie was calling the shots now. She hadn't
worked for a family practitioner all these years without
learning a thing or two about handling people. Male, female, rich, poor, young or old, they were all the same when
they were sick and scared. She stopped in Odessa for a
chicken sandwich and a glass of iced tea, placed a call to
her parents' downtown loft in Winston-Salem and happened to catch her father in. Even though she disapproved
of their lifestyles and some of the wild company they kept,
she worried about them.

"Daddy? I'm in a place out in Texas called Odessa. It's
not too far from Royal, so I guess I'll be getting in late this
afternoon. Are you and Mama going to be home for a
while? I worry about you when you're on the road."

"We're heading out for Nashville come morning. I've
got a big craft show this weekend, and the Possums are
going to make a demo."

"Oh. Well, call me when you know where you'll be

staying, all right? I gave Mama Aunt Manie's number. And remember to take your pills with you, and don't forget to walk at least a mile a day. I know it'll be hot, but if you set out first thing in the morning—I know, I love you, too, Daddy. You be sure and go with Mama to those clubs, y'hear? You know what kind of people hang out in those places.''

Callie didn't even know herself, not firsthand, but she'd heard things and read things, and her mama wasn't exactly famous for her common sense. She had to trust her father to look after them both, which didn't give her a whole lot of confidence, but she didn't know what else to do. They were both in their middle fifties, but neither of them had a lick of common sense.

Had she remembered to bring Grandpop's old photo albums?

She had. They were packed with the tube of Moravian cookies and the Moravian sugar cake, which was squashed and probably starting to mold, but it had seemed like a good idea at the time. Reminders of home, of childhood. It couldn't hurt.

Lordy, she was tired. She'd never driven any farther than Raleigh, and now here she was, striking out across the country like a pioneer. Not that the interstate was any wagon trail. Not that her little red car was any covered wagon, either, but all the same, she felt proud of herself for setting out to rescue an elderly relative in need.

The Riley women—at least those who'd been born Rileys—might be short on looks and weird on names, but according to Grandpop, they had never lacked for gumption when something needed doing.

And Callie had convinced herself that Manie needed rescuing. She had the house all ready. She had taken her time looking for a new job after Doc retired, knowing she'd be heading west for a week or so, but as soon as they were back and settled in, she'd set out and find something that suited her.

Hank was tired when he got back from Midland. The unscheduled trip to his corporate headquarters, as it turned out, had been timely. He had an outstanding board of directors, but as Badge One, he occasionally found it necessary to question what he considered a risky move. Nine times out of ten, he was proved right. The tenth time served to keep him humble.

Greg Hunt was standing by the massive fireplace under the life-size portrait of old Tex Langley when Hank walked in. There was a private entrance to the second floor, but it was seldom used. The two men met in the middle of the room.

"Got a minute?"

"Sure, come on upstairs." A close friend, Greg also served as his personal attorney, but Hank had a feeling this was about something entirely different. "You mentioned a situation. What's up?" He led the way toward the broad staircase. There was an elevator, but like the private entrance, it was seldom used.

"I'd better fill you in on the background first, then we can take it from there."

Hank poured his friend a drink, lit his own cigar and settled in to listen. He'd learned a long time ago that a moment of distraction during a briefing could spell disaster down the road.

"You remember my mentioning a woman named Anna?"

"Real looker? You had something pretty heavy going with her a while back? Family's European and big on rules?"

"Yeah, well I forgot to mention her family name. She's Anna von Oberland, of the Osterhaus von Oberlands. Crowned heads of a small European country. They're pretty big on arranged marriages."

"The hell you say. You're marrying into *royalty?*" Hank stumped out his cigar and leaned forward.

"If it were that easy, there wouldn't be a problem. They've got her in exile. I'm not even sure how she managed to get a call through, but thank God she did."

Hank waited. Greg was a lawyer. The information would emerge in the proper form, at the proper time.

"You've heard of Ivan the Terrible?"

Hank nodded. Greg scowled. "From what I hear, this guy who's determined to marry her is a dead ringer. Prince Ivan Striksky of Asterland, who's interested in expanding his holdings any way he can. Marrying Anna is easier and cheaper than a full-fledged invasion. Did I mention she has a son? She's also the guardian of her late sister's twins, which is probably going to mean a separate mission as I understand they're being held in another location. Getting all four of them out of the country is going to take some tricky maneuvering and a whole lot of luck."

"Count me in."

Greg drained his glass, sighed and leaned back in his chair.

"I already have. I'll get back to you after I talk to the others."

For a long time after Greg left, Hank sat tilted back in his favorite chair, booted feet on the windowsill, staring out the window as another hot day drained from the colorless sky. Aside from the creak of his chair, the only sound to be heard was the quiet whisper of cold air feeding through the elaborate system of ductwork.

A situation?

Hell, it was a full-blown technodrama. Romeo and Juliet out of Indiana Jones.

At thirty-two, Greg Hunt was nearly eight years Hank's junior. The man was brilliant, experienced, old enough and smart enough to avoid trouble of the female variety. This Anna of his must be something special. With three kids, yet.

He only hoped she was worth it. They'd left it with the understanding that Greg would consult with Sterling Churchill, Forrest Cunningham and Greg's younger brother, Blake, who was into cloak-and-dagger stuff for the feds. All five men, Hank included, were ex-military. It was one of the things they had in common, besides being highly successful in their individual fields.

Hank had assured Greg of his support, both financial and otherwise. Talk of undertaking a mission brought back a rash of old memories. For the first time in years, Hank felt the familiar surge of excitement, as if he were back with the First Battalion of the 160th Special Ops, being briefed for another black SOF mission.

His career with the military had been the most rewarding period of his entire life. Never before or since had he felt so fully alive. He might even have made the service a permanent career except for the confluence of several events, including his father's death, a crisis in the oil industry and the crash that had landed him in a Turkish hospital with a flock of surgeons squabbling over whether to do a chop job or try to patch up his mangled left leg.

The truth was, he missed it.

Hank had been eighteen when he'd enlisted. Reckless, resentful and still raw from his aborted marriage. Toting a redwood-size chip on his shoulder, he'd been determined to prove something—God knows what—to his old man.

Instead he'd proved something to himself. Now, some twenty-one years later, he knew who he was, what he was made of and what he was capable of achieving, either as a part of a team or on his own.

And none of it had anything to do with the fortune amassed by previous generations of Langleys.

Of the five people Hank trusted most in the world, four were ex-military and Cattleman's Club members, like himself. The fifth person with whom he would trust his life was Romania Riley. Prim, scrappy Miss Manie, a woman who smelled like lavender and who could throw the fear of God into the club's two-hundred-fifty-pound ex-marine chef with one look over the gold rim of her bifocals. The lady might drive him nuts on occasion, but she did it with the best intentions in the world.

As if his thoughts had summoned her, there came a familiar rap on his door. Hank managed to lower his feet a moment before Miss Manie marched into the room with that familiar look that invariably spelled trouble.

"Now, you're not going to like what I'm about to tell you, but just listen and don't interrupt until I'm done, all right?"

"If it's about—"

"Hush. I haven't even started yet."

Hank hushed. When she was done, he decided she'd been right. He didn't like it. Naturally he started arguing. "Look, just go ahead and take off as long as you need, you haven't had a vacation in years. Your brother's funeral last fall didn't count. Just get me someone down from the main office before you go, okay? Helen will do just fine."

"Helen's not going to drive all the way from Midland every day just to—"

"She can put up in staff's quarters for the duration."

"What, and leave her family behind?"

"Helen's got family?"

Manie shook her head, causing her bifocals to slide down her long, thin nose. "I declare, if I didn't know better, I'd think you didn't have a speck of decency in you. You don't know doodle-squat about all the folks who work their fingers to the bone for you."

"Maybe not, but I pay 'em damned well. And I do know Helen can suck data out of a computer faster than anyone else on my payroll."

"That may be, but did you know she has two sons and a husband, and teaches Sunday School at the First Baptist Church? Did you know—"

"Manie, get to the point. What does all this have to do with your niece?"

"Great-niece. She's all the family I've got left in the world, poor little thing."

When Manie put on her "poor lonesome me" act, it was time to take cover. "Fine. Or sorry, depending on your sentiments. Is the kid weaned yet? Do I need to hire a nanny?"

"Have you heard a single word I've said?"

"Enough to know you want me to baby-sit while you go up to Midland. Have you and Helen planned a big shopping spree or something?" The two women had kept in touch even after Helen had transferred to headquarters after Hank's father's death.

Manie made a sound that was part snort, part huff. He used to try to reproduce it as a kid, but he'd never been able to come close. "What I want is for you to listen," she snapped. "Now, I've put off this surgery for—"

"Surgery! What surgery? You didn't say anything about surgery!"

"I just did. Now hush up and listen."

"What kind of surgery? I can fly you to Austin—"

"I don't want you to fly me to Austin, I've got a perfectly good doctor in Midland, and she's scheduled me for next Friday morning at seven, which gives Callie just enough time to get settled and learn how we do things around here." She said it all without giving him a chance to get a word in, and then glared at him over her spectacles, daring him to argue.

"Callie?"

"My great-niece. I just finished telling you all about her, didn't you hear a single word I said?"

He'd heard it all, only he was having trouble collating all the data. "Just back up a minute, will you? First, I want to know the name of your doctor. Next, I want to know exactly what she told you, and dammit, I want to know why you never mentioned it before. Hell, I thought you just wanted a vacation. How long have you known about this? Why didn't you say something before now? Does it—" He scowled and shoved back the thick, gray-spangled hair that fell over his tanned forehead. "Here, sit down, take my chair. Want me to get you some water?" He hit the intercom button that connected him to his chef's office. "Mouse, send up a pot of tea and whatever the hell goes with tea. Crackers, cookies—whatever. It's for Miss Manie. You know what she likes."

Everyone knew what Miss Manie liked. She was an institution at the club. A roughneck's kid his father had taken in out of the oil fields and raised like his own daughter. Outspoken, occasionally outrageous, she'd earned the respect of everyone in town, even the women she called floozies. They might not like her, but they sure as hell respected her.

"Now, tell me what this is all about." He squatted before her. It damned near killed him, but he needed to see her eyes. Taking her knotty-fingered, blue-veined hands in his, he said, "Manie, sweetheart, level with me. I want to know everything—diagnosis, prognosis, treatment—whatever you know, I need to know. We're going to beat this thing, I promise. No way am I going to let anything happen to my Manie. Now what is it?"

She sighed, and he braced himself for the worst. He'd get her the finest specialists in Texas. In the U.S. In the world. What good was money if it couldn't help the ones you loved?

"If you must know, it's nothing at all serious. Just a simple repair that should have been done years ago."

"Repair what? What's broke?"

She snatched her hands from his and clapped them to her withered cheeks. "Oh, for mercy's sake, it's called female trouble," she hissed. "Now, let's get down to brass tacks, young man. Callie will be here late this afternoon, and I'm planning to bring her into the office tomorrow. She's smart as a whip, she'll be able to take over without a speck of trouble. By Thursday I'll be—"

"Whoa, back up again, honey. Take over what?"

If there was one thing Manie Riley was good at, it was coercion. Done politely, there wasn't a single thing wrong with a bit of gentle blackmail to her way of thinking, not when it was done for the good of all concerned.

And this certainly was. All she needed was a little nip and tuck to keep her from traipsing to the bathroom every fifteen minutes. What Hank needed was a decent woman to save him from all those floozies who judged a man by the size of his bankroll instead of the size of his heart, while her Callie...

Well, Callie needed a man. Some women didn't. Manie had thought, until recently, that she herself didn't need one, either, but then, live and learn, they said.

They also said there was no fool like an old fool, but that was another matter.

"Gracious, are you sure about this?" Callie exclaimed. Pushing away her plate, she tried to focus on all the lists her great-aunt had presented along with the sweet potato pie. She was still reeling from the trip, amazed that she'd actually managed to get here after driving for what seemed forever.

Royal was a tiny little town, hardly more than a speck on the map. She'd been afraid she'd miss it and wander around forever in the most desolate country she'd ever seen, but suddenly, there it was, green as a pool table, right in the middle of a desert. No wonder they had all those windmills going full tilt day and night, hauling water up from way underground. It must take a zillion gallons just to keep all the lawns watered.

"Wake up, don't you dare fall asleep at the table. Now pay attention, I promised Hank I'd bring you in tomorrow and show you the ropes."

"Aunt Manie, I'm not very good with a computer and my bookkeeping is probably not what he's used to. Honestly, are you sure—?"

"I'm sure. Secretaries aren't what they were in my day. What with all these machines people use nowadays, they're practically obsolete, but don't worry about that, what you'll be is more like a personal assistant. If you worked for that crochety old man I met at Wharrie's funeral, you can work for anybody. My Hank's a sweet boy. All he needs is someone to screen his calls and keep folks from pestering him for donations, or papas wanting to take him home to meet their daughters, or these jumped-up schoolteachers wanting him to endow a chair at some university. You'll be taking care of his personal needs, that's all."

Callie's eyes widened, but before her imagination could shift into overdrive, her great-aunt continued, "Now, I've listed everything you need to know right here. What calls to put through right off, which ones to stall, who to let in, who to keep out, who to interrupt if they stay more than ten minutes. This list here is the numbers of his favorite restaurants for making reservations. If he's taking a woman, he'll likely take her to Claire's, but if it's one of his friends, they'll go to the Royal Diner for hot dogs and coconut pie. The Royal don't take reservations. Here's the number for the florist, the cleaners and the pharmacy where he gets his migraine medicine. He won't need it often, but when he does, he'll need it right quick. They deliver. Here's his private pilot's number and—oh, yes, here's the phone number where I'll be staying once I get out of the clinic."

Merciful heavens, Callie felt as if she'd run head-on into a Texas tornado, which couldn't be much worse than the Carolina variety, only after a four-day drive, she wasn't in any condition to put up much of a fight. "Yes, but—"

"I can't tell you how much it means to know I can go off with a clear conscience, I've been putting it off for so long."

"But, Aunt Manie—"

"This way, I can rest easy about my plants. Every third day for those in the east window, every day for the south side. I've left instructions in the kitchen."

"Yes, but—" Callie tried again. Manie had hit her with this thing before she'd even opened her suitcase. "Shouldn't I go with you? To the clinic, I mean? I could stay with you—even working in Doc Teeter's office, I learned how to—"

"Pshaw. No point in turnin' a real nurse out of her job. With you looking after things here, I can rest easy in my mind. You'll be a darn sight more good to me here than you will in Midland. Besides, I've got plenty of friends there.''

They went back a forth a few more times, but youth and determination were no match for age, experience and a conniving turn of mind. Callie knew when to give in. Her own plans would just have to wait. ''All right, I'll do my best, but don't blame me if your Mr. Langley sends me packing. I know a lot about men, and—''

Manie snorted again.

''—and one thing for sure, they don't like any changes in their routine. Doc Teeter is the sweetest man alive, but just let me slip up and send in the first patient before he finishes his second cup of coffee, and he'll growl all day.''

''You won't have to worry about that with Hank. He'll bend over backward not to cause you a speck of trouble. Like I said, he's the sweetest boy in the world.''

Callie, shoulders slumping, eyelids at half-mast, had her doubts about that, but there wasn't much she could do about it. The arrangements had already been made. Her aunt needed her, if only to water her precious plants and set her mind at ease so she could heal properly.

And after this, she thought smugly, Manie was going to owe her. ''All right then, if your sweet boy agrees, I'll do my best.''

Manie beamed. Face flushed with pleasure and two glasses of blackberry wine, she looked far younger than the sixty-nine years she admitted to. ''I'm just as sorry as I can be the way things worked out, but when I scheduled my operation, I wasn't sure you'd actually come to visit.''

''Yes, well…I guess it worked out for the best. Just remember, once the operation's done, we're going to have a serious talk about the future. I've had a wonderful idea, and I can't wait to tell you all about it.''

The elderly woman nodded, and then nodded again.

Leaning over, Callie peered up into her face and saw that she was dozing.

Well. She was pretty tired, herself, after driving practically nonstop all the way across the country. A few hours of sleep in a series of cheap motels hardly counted as rest.

Hank stared morosely at the blinking red light on his answering machine, tempted to ignore it. Discipline took over. Besides, it might be Manie. He still wasn't convinced she hadn't made light of her illness just to keep him from worrying.

The first message was from Pansy. She wanted him to call her the minute he got back to town. The next two were from headquarters, about some drilling rights that were coming up for renewal. Another one was from a candidate in the upcoming election, wanting money. He happened to know the man was the biggest crook in six counties, not that that meant he wouldn't be an effective politician, but all the same, he'd pass on this one.

The last message was from Manie. "Hank, I'll be bringing Callie by in the morning to show her around and introduce her to the staff. She's tired, so we might not be in before ten, but I want you to promise me you'll be nice to her." As if he'd be anything else to one of Manie's relatives. "She's a hard worker and real good with people. Give her a day or two and she'll do just fine. I'll be bringing you a slice of my sweet potato pie, too, so save room for it."

Sighing, Hank dropped into his chair, raked his fingers through his hair and wondered, not for the first time, if he was too old and beat-up to get back into the service.

Three

How could anyone perspire with a ceiling fan going full blast? Callie wiped the sweat from her eyes and plopped her aunt's iron back on the stove to cool. She hung her white camp shirt over a chair, folded away the ironing board, and called down the hall to where Manie was watching the morning news on TV.

"I'll be ready in ten minutes, all right?"

"Take your time, I told Hank we'd be late."

Callie didn't want to take her time, she wanted to get it over with. Manie's Hank might be a paragon of all virtues, but no man liked having his routine disrupted. Bringing someone new on the job with little or no notice was the sort of thing Doc Teeter had always hated. Even Grandpop, the sweetest man in the world, used to grumble when she happened to call during a Lawrence Welk rerun or his nightly bowl of ice cream and the Channel 8 news. Women were adaptable because they had to be, but men were creatures of habit.

She did the best she could with what she had to work with. Blond hair. At least, in the summer it was blond. At least the top layer was blond. Underneath, and in the wintertime, it was more the color of tree bark. She'd had it cut really short just before she'd come west, because it was too thick and too curly to manage otherwise. Her eyes were too big, too pale, but fortunately, her glasses hid the faint shadows that always seemed to show up just when she wanted to look her best.

As for her clothes, they were neat, clean and serviceable. She'd been told more than a few times that she had absolutely no sense of style, but as it was her mother who'd told her, she'd taken it with a grain of salt. Any fifty-two-year-old woman who wore fringed miniskirts, cowboy boots, satin blouses and half a pound of silver dangling from each ear the way her mother did these days didn't have a whole lot of room to criticize.

Her father was just as bad. The day he'd turned in his resignation he'd given his suits to Goodwill and held a ceremonial necktie-burning. Since then all he wore were torn blue jeans, waffle-stomping boots and risqué T-shirts. On really dressy occasions, he added beads and an earring.

Callie would be the first to admit she was dull as ditchwater. It was a good thing somebody in her family was, or else who would take care of them all when they were too old to run wild any longer?

By the time they entered the Texas Cattleman's Club, Callie had gnawed off a thumbnail. Why couldn't Manie have worked for a nice, respectable family doctor in a small suburban clinic instead of a high-powered millionaire in a fancy gentleman's club in a plush little oasis in the middle of a desert that bristled with windmills and oil derricks? Callie felt as if she'd wandered onto a movie set. She wasn't at all sure she could cope.

Well, of course she could cope. She always had, hadn't she?

All the same, she stopped dead in her tracks, her sensible beige pumps sinking into a richly colored rug, and stared at the vast, high-ceilinged, dark-paneled room filled with heavy leather furniture, a massive fireplace and decorated with rows and rows of huge oil paintings, animal heads and antique gun displays.

She forgot to breathe, and then breathed too deeply, inhaling lemon oil, floor wax and the essence of roughly a hundred years' of cigar smoke and brandy.

"Come along, honey, the stairs are right over here. I reckon we could've taken the elevator, but nobody ever does."

Callie swallowed hard. Her blouse was stuck to her back. The place was chilled down to goose bump territory, but her palms were wet and her mouth was dry, and she knew, she just knew, that Mr. Langley was going to take one look at her and realize that she was scared silly and way, way out of her element.

You can do this, Caledonia Riley. You survived your parents' midlife crisis, Doc's retirement and Grandpop's passing. You can do anything you set your mind to, and besides, Aunt Manie's old and sick, and she's counting on you.

Callie knew her role in life. She was a caretaker. A looker-after. She might not have a college degree, but she was real good with people. She lived by the Golden Rule. The one about doing unto others, etc. If she could do it without hurting feelings, she always spoke her mind to avoid misunderstandings.

Only this time she hadn't...not completely. At least,

she'd told her aunt she wanted to take her back home for a nice, long visit. Which was more of an understatement than an outright lie.

Manie's office was a cul-de-sac near the head of the stairs, consisting of a rosewood desk, an oak filing cabinet and a French provincial library table holding a stack of books, a copier, a fax machine, a telephone and an old manual typewriter. Across the way was a tall window bracketed by heavy linen drapes and walnut louvered blinds folded back to display a row of African violets.

There were two wing chairs upholstered in a dainty chintz print, but instead of stopping there, Manie crossed to the massive walnut door a few feet beyond and rapped sharply. Without waiting for a response, she opened the door and waved Callie into the lion's den.

"Here she is, here's my Callie. Honey, meet Hank Langley. He's just as sweet as he can be, so don't let that scowl of his fool you."

It was a good thing she was wearing panty hose. That was the only thing that kept her knees from buckling as the big, dark, unsmiling man rose from another of the massive leather-covered chairs. How many cows had been sacrificed for this man's comfort?

More to the point, how many secretaries had been sacrificed on the altar of his personal convenience?

"Say hello to your new employer," her aunt urged. Callie must have made a sound of some sort, because the scowl disappeared.

"Miss Riley." Her new employer nodded gravely.

"M-Mr. Langley," she said, trying to sound as if she weren't sweating like a horse under her neat cotton blouse and tan poplin skirt. *This* was Hank Langley? Her aunt's sweet, sensitive boy? The man who wouldn't swat a fly if he could open a window and let it out?

No way. This man was a...

Well, she didn't know what he was, but he was no sweet, harmless little boy. She'd heard all about Texas men. According to those songs her mother played on the kitchen radio and sang along with, they rode harder, drank more, made love better and broke more hearts than any other two-legged creature in the known world. The songs didn't even begin to do justice to the real thing.

Oh, my....

"Does she need anything? A glass of water?" His voice was just like the rest of him. Deep, dark and dangerously masculine.

"It's all that driving," her great-aunt replied. "I reckon her poor body's still stuck on Eastern Standard Time."

They were talking over her head as if she weren't even there. Callie took a deep breath and said, "If you think I can do the job, Mr. Langley, I'm perfectly willing to give it my best effort. If not—"

"No problem, Miss, uh—Riley. Your aunt vouches for you."

He was a full head taller than she was, but then, so was almost everyone else. His hair was thick and so dark it absorbed the light, except for a few glints of silver scattered evenly throughout. His eyes were blue. So were hers, only where his were the color of one of those deep blue mineral oil bottles, hers were more the color of a sun-faded denim shirt.

They talked some more, at least Mr. Langley and her aunt did. Callie was having trouble trying to sift through so many new impressions and get her brain back in working order. Evidently it had gotten scrambled during the trip, because the thoughts that were racing through her mind like a pair of courting squirrels spiraling round and round a poplar tree were the last thing she needed at this point in her life.

"—sent word to the committee head about the meeting next week—"

"—cancel the tickets and call—"

"—deliver tomorrow. Callie can sign for it, I told them all about her."

Told who what? Callie wondered. That she was here in body, but her brain was suffering jet lag?

Well, car lag. Four days of driving, living on fast food and diet colas, her mind busy framing arguments that would convince her aunt to forget Texas, move back home to Carolina and let Callie take care of her, produced more or less the same results.

"I'm sure you'll do just fine, Miss, uh—Callie. Manie won't have a thing to worry about, will she?"

Wordlessly she nodded, then shook her head. "No, sir."

He looked as if he might be suffering from acute dyspepsia. She'd never had that particular effect on a man before. The truth was, she'd never had much effect at all, not being the type of woman men went wild over. Wholesome was about the nicest thing that had ever been said about her looks. This man, like all the others, had glanced at her once, shaken her hand, and two minutes after she left he'd have forgotten both her name and her face.

She stood outside his door a few minutes later, waiting for her aunt to finish her conversation, and thought, The Invisible Woman Meets the Invincible Man. It sounded like one of those high-tech movies, full of sound and fury and special effects.

She was hallucinating. She told herself it had to be something in the water. Because for one split second when she'd gazed up at the man she was going to be working for for more than a week, she'd felt as if someone had struck a note that resonated on her inner tuning fork, the one her mother the musician swore all women had. Sort of like meeting someone for the first time and feeling as if you'd met them somewhere before. None of which made a speck of sense.

"We'd better get you something to eat before you pass out," her aunt said, emerging from the inner sanctum a moment later. "You didn't eat enough breakfast to keep a grasshopper alive."

Hank tilted his favorite chair, lifted his feet to the windowsill and stared out at the colorless sky, visualizing dark gray clouds rolling in from the northwest. He imagined himself in the cockpit of one of the old MH-60 Blackhawks, his field of vision transformed by night-vision goggles. For some crazy reason he was feeling the same familiar rush, the heady mixture of determination and invincibility, he used to feel when he first headed out on a mission.

If anyone here had a mission, it was Manie. She'd insisted it was no big deal, but he'd had his people check things out, just to be sure. He'd talked with both her primary care physician and the surgeon. Dr. Schwartz had explained the simple procedure over the phone, assuring Hank that it was routine, and that Miss Riley, who had the constitution of a woman half her age, would breeze through it. He rarely pulled rank—rarely had to. In this case, however, he wanted the entire medical community to know that Romania Riley had friends in high places.

That done, all he had to do now was put up with Little Miss Muffet for the duration, without hurting her feelings. She looked as if a misplaced sneeze would do the trick, in which case Miss Manie would carve out his liver and feed it to the crows. She'd always been a tiger when it came to protecting those she considered her own, Hank included. A great-niece, even one with all the spunk of a day-old lamb, would probably come under the same heading.

The rest of the day went surprisingly well, possibly because Carrie, or Callie, or whatever her name was, had Miss Manie hovering over her shoulder, checking out every move. Hank was almost afraid to step outside the door.

Even with his door shut, he could hear the constant murmur of voices. The phone rang incessantly with last-minute adjustments in the plans for the annual ball.

She looked about twelve years old. Had to be older than that, though, because Manie said she'd worked as a secretary for the past six years.

Carrie. Callie? What the hell was her name, anyway? One of those crazy names like Romania?

Carolina? That would make it Carrie.

"Carrie," he called on the intercom, "would you step in here a minute, please?"

Colorless. Drab was another way of putting it, Hank thought as he watched her come in. She'd make a great bank robber. Two minutes after the getaway, not a single witness would be able to describe her.

Her voice was something else. Soft, husky, but surprisingly firm. "Yes, sir, how may I help you?"

"Listen, you're not a salesclerk, and you're not a waitress."

"No, sir."

"Is that how you addressed your former employer?"

"No, sir."

"Good. Then you can address me the same way."

She tilted her head, ever so slightly. "You want me to call you Doc Teeter?"

"Oh, hell." Hank could have sworn he saw a gleam

behind those hideous glasses of hers. "Call me Hank. Out here in Texas, we're not so formal as you folks in the high-and-mighty East."

He was right. It had been a gleam. What's more, the corner of her lips were twitching under a thin layer of lipstick so pale it hardly rated as color. Nice mouth, though. Generous, with a slight upward tilt and a full lower lip. It was the real thing, too. No silicon. No woman who dressed the way this one did would go for a silicon job. Waste of money.

"Did you buzz me earlier, sir? Hank? I'm not quite sure which light is which yet, they're not labeled. Aunt Manie went downstairs to talk to the kitchen people before she leaves, so she might be the one who buzzed me. Do you think she wants me to go downstairs?"

"Tell me, Carrie, do I look like a mind reader to you?"

"Not at all, you look like a— That is, no, sir. Hank. And it's Callie, not Carrie, but you could always call me Miss Riley."

Tilting his chair again, he laced his hands behind his head. It was like playing ball with a kitten. Toss it out, just to watch her swat at it. She was such an earnest little thing, he was tempted to tell her to lighten up. "Call Claire's, will you? Reservations for two, at nine."

She gave a jerky little nod and scuttled out the door as if she was afraid he might lunge at her. Did she really think he was that hard up?

No way. He'd lay odds her Doc Teeter had never laid a hand on her, either, and not just because in today's world, it would probably spell the end of his career.

Funny how different they were. Manie, for all she was prim as a picket fence, had a wicked sense of humor. He'd a lot rather take her to the Cattleman's Ball than Pansy or

Bianca. At least with Manie, he didn't have to be on his guard every minute.

Speaking of which, unless he could come up with a good excuse, he was going to have to make a decision. About the ball, as well as the other. Both women were practically breathing down his neck.

With one or two minor exceptions, the rest of day proceeded without a hitch. At half past one, Hank called downstairs and had one of the boys run down to the Royal Diner for chili and pie. He was on the phone with his broker for the fifteen minutes it took him to eat. After that, he met with an informal committee of geologists and engineers. They spent a couple of hours going over the results of the last 3-D seismological reports.

Not until after they'd filed out did it occur to him that he'd spent half the time listening to their assessments and the other half wondering if Callie was ready yet to throw in the towel.

And then Greg called. "I'm having some problems with Forrest. He's convinced I'll be recognized if I try to storm the castle. Hell, man, it's been four years since I've even been to that part of the world."

"All it takes is one jerk with a long memory to blow the whole mission. What about Blake, could he go in?"

"He'll be on a separate mission, if things go as planned. The twins are only a few months old. Getting into where they're being kept is going to be dicey. With Blake's training, he's the best candidate for that particular part of Alpha."

The mission had been given a name, which somehow made it all the more real.

God, the adrenaline was already flowing, and things were only in rough-draft mode.

"I can still fly a plane," Hank reminded him.

"I've slated you for home-base coordinator. It's imperative we have someone with a cool head directing things from a central position. If things get messy and we have to improvise, someone's got to lead the band."

"I'll dust off my baton," Hank said dryly. As the oldest member of the crew, he was the logical choice. Nevertheless, he resented being left behind. He wondered if Greg had given any thought to what was going to happen once he extracted Anna and her brood from wherever they were being held. Ivan the Territorial didn't sound like the kind of guy to willingly share his toys.

Two minutes after Greg hung up, Pansy called again, wanting to know if he needed help with last-minute arrangements for the ball, as her plans for a shopping trip to L.A. had fallen through and she had some time on her hands.

He managed to put her off with some trumped up excuse. Then, leaning back in his chair, he swore softly. He'd trade a Middle East oil crisis and a couple of hostile takeover attempts anyday for the personal decision he was facing.

Over the past six months or so, he'd narrowed the choices down to Pansy and Bianca. Pansy didn't like kids. Hank didn't particularly care to have his child raised solely by hired nursemaids. Besides which, Pansy would bore him out of his gourd if he spent much time with her.

Not that that was a requisite. Marriage, at least in his social and financial circles, was pretty much a mutually beneficial business arrangement, drawn up by lawyers on both sides and sanctioned for the duration by the state. Togetherness wasn't a part of the deal. Both women knew the score.

Bianca liked kids. Claimed to, at least. She also had a sense of humor. Any woman in her middle thirties who could giggle hard enough to split a seam had to have a sense of humor...didn't she?

Oh, hell, maybe he'd better look around some more.

Better yet, he could drop the whole thing. So what if he was the end of the line? It was no big deal. Maybe he'd leave everything to the IRS, since they'd end up getting the lion's share anyway. That ought to open up a major fault line on Wall Street.

Feeling restless, he paced the room that he called his office, which was roughly the size of the billiard room downstairs. When his leg began to protest, he dropped into his desk chair again, swiveled it around and stared out the window, willing a cold front to push through. Willing the hot, dry wind to stop blowing and the rains to start falling. Willing the call from Germany he was expecting to come through so that he could get out and work off some tension.

He was too old to be racing a dirt bike over sand hills, but he did it anyway, miles out in the country where nobody could see him and claim he was acting like a damned fool, risking his neck.

He wondered what Callie would think if she could see him racing hell-bent out in the middle of nowhere.

And then he wondered why he was even wondering. Why he wasted valuable time thinking about a meek little dab of a female who looked as if she was scared to death he was going to jump her bones.

Idly he wondered if anyone ever had.

He was still grinning over the thought of Miss Manie's little lamb in an X-rated situation when the ruckus erupted just outside his door. Then the door burst open and Pansy presented herself. She was in a snit over something, that much was obvious.

Carrie-Callie was riding her tail, looking frantic. "Ma'am, I can't—Mr. Langley said he wasn't to be disturbed, so if you'll just— Please, ma'am, won't you let me announce you?''

"Who *is* this creature?" Pansy demanded.

"Didn't Manie introduce you? This is her niece, um—"

"Miss Callie Riley," Callie filled in for her boss, who had obviously forgotten her name. "Actually, it's Caledonia," she said, lifting her jaw a fraction. See if you can remember *that*, Hanky Panky, she thought with grim amusement.

Pansy blinked at her, then turned back to Hank. "Vince just invited me to join him in Houston for a cruise to the Virgin Islands. I reminded him about the Cattleman's Ball. I haven't missed it in years, and this year—"

"Why not take him up on the offer? Lie around in the sun a few weeks, let old Vince wait on you, it'll do him good."

"But the ball—?"

"We'll manage without you for once. Callie'll help. She's going as my partner this year, did I tell you?"

Callie opened her mouth and remembered a few seconds later to shut it. She was doing *what?*

As his *what?*

"Oh, for God's sake, secretaries don't count. You can take your whole damned staff for all I care, but—"

"It'll be Callie's first ball," he said softly. A little too softly. "I mean to make it a special occasion."

They stared laser beams at each other in a silent battle of wills. Callie wanted to sink through the floor, but as it was solid oak, every plank more than a foot wide and pegged down securely, it probably wasn't going to happen.

"I'll call you when I get back," the tall, elegant beauty said tightly. After sending Callie a look that would blister paint, she left, head high, invisible smoke, Callie was quite sure, pouring from both ears.

"Would you care to tell me what that was all about—sir?"

"I thought I just did. What part didn't you understand?"

"The part about the ball."

"Annual affair, benefits local charities. Manie filled you in, didn't she? I need you to go with me, that's all. Manie's done it any number of times, she'll tell you what's expected. You'll need a dress. Pick out something and put it on my account."

When pigs flew. "Going to balls wasn't mentioned in my job description." Mentally she skimmed down the lists her aunt had given her. She was certain there'd been no mention of attending any social functions. Certainly not a ball. She didn't even have a pumpkin, much less a fairy godmother, and she wasn't about to charge anything on his account, not so much as a pair of socks.

Aunt Manie had supper ready when Callie got back to the neat little bungalow three blocks off Main Street, having left in the middle of the afternoon to get started packing for her stay at the clinic.

Callie felt as if she'd barely managed to get out of the lion's den with her skin intact. "Aunt Manie, do you know what he—"

"I'm back in the kitchen. Go wash up while I stick the rolls in the microwave to heat. 'Twon't take but a second, these newfangled ovens can ruin food fast as they can cook it."

Callie washed her hands, splashed cold water on her face, ran a comb through her hair and felt marginally refreshed. She was as stiff and sore as if she'd had every muscle in her body clenched for the past few hours, which was little less than the truth.

"Do you know what he did?" She started in as soon as she'd stirred her iced tea.

"What who did? Have some butter beans."

"Your precious boy, that's who. He invited me—no, he didn't invite me, he *ordered* me—well, he didn't even do that, he just told that Ostrich woman I was going to the ball with him."

"Estrich. Mmm, I was wondering how he was going to get out of it. She's been pestering him, both her and Bianca, ever since last year's ball. Been competing over one thing or another ever since they were in grade school. I swear, half the things they fight over they don't really want, they just can't stand for the other one to get a jump on them."

"Wait a minute—how he's going to get out of what? Didn't you hear what I said? He expects me to go to a ball! Aunt Manie, I don't go to balls. I've never even been to a dance except for one square dance out at the old Polirosa in Tobaccoville."

"Nothing to it. I've been to dozens of balls. I even line-danced once just to prove I wasn't over the hill."

"Yes, well I'm not over it, either, but that doesn't mean I—"

"Here, have a helping of these sweet potatoes. I'd like to borrow that suitcase of yours if you don't mind. Never did get the latch fixed on mine. Besides, mine's genuine cowhide. Weighs a ton."

They talked some more, but when Callie turned out the kitchen light an hour later, nothing had been settled. She was still going to have to go to that darned ball or come up with a good reason why she couldn't. According to her aunt, her boy was at a dangerous age, feeling his biological clock ticking away.

"I thought only women had biological clocks."

"Yes, well...men have a longer shelf life, but that

doesn't mean they can't do something silly, just because they're a few weeks away from a certain birthday."

"And Hank is?"

Manie gave her a knowing look. "Those two females, Pansy and Bianca, have been doing their darnedest for years to trap that poor boy into marrying them."

"Aunt Manie, he's hardly a boy." Lordy, anything less boyish would be hard to imagine. He even had *her* hormones sizzling like batter in a skillet full of hot fat. She'd watched Doc plunge needles into the quaking flesh of some of the primest male behinds in Yadkin County without the least twinge of interest.

"That may be, but with that pair breathing down his neck, one false step and his goose is cooked. He deserves better than that."

"He's certainly old enough to watch his step. He doesn't need either of us to watch it for him. Besides, I don't have anything suitable to wear. I only brought enough for a week. Washable stuff. Shorts, skirts and a few blouses. And only two pairs of shoes, these pumps for Sunday and the sandals I wore traveling."

"Make a list of what you need and we'll go shopping after supper before I leave."

"We'll do nothing of the kind. I have to work, and your friend's coming to drive you to the clinic. If I need to shop, I can do it myself. I've been buying my own clothes ever since I was in the fourth grade."

Manie's look spoke volumes, which Callie chose to ignore. She felt like throwing herself on her aunt's flat bosom and pleading with her not to leave, which was alarming in itself, because Callie wasn't the type to lean on anyone. She was a leaning post herself. Always had been. She fully intended to play the same role in her aunt's golden years, only first they had to get through this surgery business, and to do that, Callie had to take over Manie's job so the poor woman wouldn't worry herself to a frazzle.

"All right, I'll look after your boy for you, and I'll water your plants and I'll go to the darned ball. You just remember, though—you owe me for this, Manie Riley, because going to balls is over and above the call of duty."

Manie only smiled.

Four

The dress was all wrong. Callie knew it as soon as she slipped it over her head, but it was too late. All the shops were closed. As rattled as she was, if she had to do it over again, she'd probably choose something even worse.

It was a prom dress, not a ball gown. Pale yellow, never her best color, with cap sleeves and a full gored skirt. She should've gone shopping before her aunt left for Midland. Manie would've known better. But she'd been trying so hard to pretend she had everything under control.

She had nothing under control, in spite of all the checklists her aunt had left her, all the checklists she'd made herself. Someone had once told her she used lists to give herself an illusion of control over life.

It wasn't working.

She heard the doorbell and gave one last tug at her low neckline, one last pat to her hair, rinsed in lemon water for the occasion, and one last thumbs-up to the frumpy looking creature in the mirror.

Yellow, for heaven's sake. Black would've been better— a woman couldn't go wrong with a little black dress. But black made her look even more washed out than yellow. Blue would've been good, but the only blue she could find in her price range was slit up to the gazoo. Not even in Texas would she expose her gazoo, not for all the Hank Langleys in the world.

Wish me luck, Aunt Manie. I'm off to protect your sensitive, vulnerable boy from all those underdressed, overpainted hussies. Thank goodness, she thought, hurrying to answer the front door, her sense of humor had survived the trip, even if her common sense had fallen by the wayside.

Hank wondered why he hadn't just sent a car and driver to pick up his secretary. What if she misunderstood this whole affair? What if she thought he was personally interested in her?

He shot his cuff and glanced at his wrist. One minute and counting. He jammed his thumb on the buzzer again. Where the hell was she? The house wasn't all that big. He should know—he'd bought it for Manie when he found out she'd been paying rent on it all these years.

He'd tried to get her to move into his father's old house, but she claimed it was big enough for an army, and besides, she wouldn't be able to set her plants around on the windowsills.

The door opened a crack and he found himself peering into an enormous silver-blue eye. "Aren't you ready yet?" he demanded, sounding more impatient than he'd intended.

"I don't think so. Why don't you just go without me? I'm not a very good dancer, anyway."

"Neither am I. Come along, Callie, grab your wrap and bag and let's go, I need to be there."

"I don't have an evening bag, I forgot to buy one."

"Fine. Stuff a hanky in your bosom and come on, will you?" He glanced at his watch again. Dammit, with Manie gone, someone needed to be there to oversee this production. He trusted his staff implicitly, but he had a feeling Murphy's Law might prevail tonight. Whatever could go wrong, would go wrong.

He heard her sigh and wondered if he should've sent her flowers. It hadn't occurred to him. That was the kind of thing Manie did for him.

But then, if he'd sent flowers, she might have misunderstood, and the last thing he needed was one more woman putting the moves on him. Not that he thought of Callie as a woman. At least, not an eligible woman. Hell, he was old enough to be her father.

Yellow. She looked like a wildflower in that getup. Not a bad stem, either, come to think of it. Unbidden, his gaze skimmed her slender lines in masculine appreciation. He cleared his throat and said, "Look, Callie, this isn't a regular date, it's a—"

"I know that," she said quietly, in that soft, oddly husky voice of hers. Texas was southern, but there was something different about that Carolina drawl.

"Yeah, well...I just didn't want you to get the wrong idea."

"I'm your employee, sir. Employees are not paid to get the wrong idea."

Was she being facetious? He glanced at her profile, checking her lips. No twitch. They had a little more color than usual, but no hint of a smile.

He couldn't read her. It was beginning to bug him, because most women were clear as glass. They wanted what he represented, even if they had to take him to get it. Even those with money wanted the power and prestige he represented. He'd managed over the years to put things into perspective so that his ego remained unscathed. Being a businessman, he understood assets and liabilities. But there were times when too many assets could become a liability.

Hank handed the keys of his car to the bartender's kid, who helped out on these occasions. Callie was still trying to deal with a bunch of petticoats when he got around to the passenger side. Obviously she wasn't used to dealing with all that extra yardage. Flushed, she looked almost pretty. In a fresh-faced, big-eyed sort of way. Not that he had any intention of telling her so. No point in taking the risk of crossing any invisible lines.

The outside of the two-and-a-half-story clubhouse was not particularly impressive. Hank liked it that way. It made the foyer's polished walnut paneling, the lush Oriental rugs and the gleaming touches of brass all the more impressive by contrast.

He tried to see the place through the eyes of a stranger, partially succeeded and gave it up as irrelevant.

"You can take your things upstairs if you want to," he said tersely, scanning the early arrivals. "Leave 'em in Manie's closet."

Her things consisted of a small tan leather purse that was all wrong with her dress, and a lightweight tan cardigan that was hardly ballroom wear. But then, neither was her gown, at least not for anyone over sixteen years old.

He watched her walk toward the stairs, bell-shaped skirts swaying around her slender hips, and felt the tug of something almost like tenderness. Protectiveness. He hoped to hell she knew how to deal with cats, because they were going to be out in full force tonight. He hadn't lived this long as a bachelor without learning a thing or two about women and the way they reacted when an innocent by-stander got between them and something they wanted. And Callie was definitely an innocent bystander.

Still thinking about her youth and obvious inexperience, he was watching her ascend the staircase when she turned and glanced over her shoulder. Their eyes met and held just a moment too long before Hank, swearing under his breath, turned away, hoping no one had noticed.

"That was real sweet of you," Pansy murmured, coming up from behind to hook both her arms in his.

"What was real sweet of me?" he asked absently, managing to keep the irritation from breaking through.

"Inviting your little secretary to the ball. She must be thrilled to pieces, poor thing."

"I thought you were off on a cruise." He freed his arm on the pretext of signaling a waiter.

"I decided I'd rather be here. Danny brought me." Danny was her first cousin, a third-generation member who seldom availed himself of the club's facilities.

"Better check his shoes for cleats before you take to the dance floor." Danny was a professional football player, good-looking, popular, but without a whole lot between the ears.

He left her there, murmuring something about making a phone call, and then, because he dreaded wading into the well-dressed mob, and because he really was worried about Manie in spite of all her reassurances, he figured he might as well go upstairs and give her a call before things started heating up.

Callie was seated in one of Manie's two wing chairs, her head back, eyes closed, fingers knotted in her lap. He'd heard of heart-shaped faces. She had one. He didn't know why he hadn't noticed before. "Hey, are you all right?" he asked softly.

Her eyes flew open. They were so large, so expressive, he couldn't imagine why she hid such an asset behind those ugly, plastic-rimmed glasses. Tonight she hadn't. "Are you wearing contacts?"

"No. I can see well enough without my glasses, I'm just more comfortable wearing them."

In other words, she hid behind them. Idly he wondered why.

"I guess I have to go downstairs, don't I?"

Considering this was *the* social event of the year, and she was here with a guy who was considered something of a catch, she didn't sound any too eager. "Yeah, I guess you do. Don't worry, they're a pretty decent bunch, for the most part. Even the few who bite have had their rabies shots. Believe me, I'm careful about that sort of thing."

She'd closed her eyes again, but her lips twitched. He found himself increasingly fascinated by the subtle way she expressed her feelings. He'd seen her smile a couple of times, but he'd never heard her laugh.

"Am I supposed to be taking notes or something? You said Aunt Manie took notes for you."

"Manie's good at forming impressions so that she can act as my sounding board when some of the newer local charities hit us up for major funding. I don't expect you to do that, you don't know these people well enough yet."

"Then what am I supposed to do?"

"What did you do for your last employer?"

"Kept his books, did his billing, ordered supplies, handled his appointments, filled out forms, reminded him about birthdays and anniversaries—nothing really complicated. Mostly it was paperwork, but sometimes if his nurse was late coming back from lunch, I stood in for her, especially when the patient was female. Doc kept forgetting what a dangerous place the world's become."

"Manie does the same sort of thing for me."

"I know. At least she said I was supposed to help protect you from overpainted, underdressed hussies who want to marry you because you're rich and well connected."

"That's plain speaking with a vengeance." He leaned back against Manie's desk, studying the woman seated before him. Could anyone be as guileless as she appeared to be? "What do you think, Callie? You up to the job?"

"Of protecting you? I think we're talking about a different kind of protection from what I'm used to. I've never seen so many gorgeous women in one place before, but I don't think they're here to bring you cookies or offer to sew on your buttons."

Hank had to laugh. Either she was even more naive than she looked, or she had a droll sense of humor. Possibly both. "Look, I'm going to give Manie a call if you want to pick up on your extension." When he brushed past to step into his office, an elusive fragrance reached out to him.

Soap? Shampoo?

Lemons. At least she wasn't trying to sweeten him up.

A few minutes later when he put down the phone, he was frowning. "She was discharged late this afternoon. Did you know anything about it?"

Callie spoke from the open doorway. "Only that she planned to go stay with a friend after she was discharged so she'd be handy for the follow-up visit."

"It's too soon. What the devil are they thinking about, letting her go this early?"

"It's a simple procedure. Still, I'm pretty sure her insurance would've paid for another night if they thought she needed it."

"Insurance bedamned, I want her back in that clinic where she'll have the kind of care she needs," he said grimly.

"Hank, her friend will look after her. Aunt Manie assured me of that when I offered to drive her to Midland."

"Just who is this friend? Have you met her?"

"Not personally, but I have her address and phone number at home. I'm planning to drive up to Midland tomorrow, so I'll meet her then."

"I'll drive you."

"You don't have to do that, I know the way. If I have any trouble locating the address, I can call and get directions."

"You don't need to be on the road in that old clunker of yours."

She bristled at that. They were both standing, Callie looking almost incandescent in pale yellow against the dark paneling. Once again Hank felt that odd wrenching sensation that could be indigestion, but probably wasn't. Lemon juice. What the devil did she do, rub a slice behind her ears?

"My car's not all that old. It's...well, it's mature, but it got me here safely without a speck of trouble."

"We'll discuss it in the morning," he growled, taking her arm, "Right now we'd better go back downstairs. Things are getting noisy."

Three hours later, things were simmering along nicely. Callie, seated at a table for two on the edge of the dance floor, could scarcely hear herself think. The rowdy, well-dressed crowd drowned out the orchestra, which played louder to be heard over the noise, which caused the ballgoers to raise their voices even more to be heard over the music.

She fanned with her handkerchief, wondering where Hank was and which of his women he was entertaining at the moment. Pansy was one of the most beautiful women she'd ever seen. She looked like a Hollywood star, or maybe a model. Bianca was shorter and laughed more, but she was just as intimidating. Her hair was the kind seen only in shampoo commercials, so thick and straight and lustrous it couldn't possibly be real.

Callie had watched him run the gauntlet of what she thought of as Dowager's Row, stopping to talk with every elderly woman present. Each one hung on to him as long as possible, knotty fingers, sparkling with diamonds, clinging to his hands, to his arm. As he moved on down the line, they put their heads together, tongues wagging fit to kick up a breeze, avid eyes following as he made his way slowly around the room.

A distinctive giggle broke the sound barrier, causing several heads to turn. Evidently Bianca was having a grand time tonight. Callie was beginning to sort out the few people she'd met. Hank was mingling, like a good host was supposed to do. Evidently he knew everyone present and intended to exchange a few words with each of them. He looked devastatingly handsome for a man who truly wasn't. At least, not by traditional standards. It had to be sex appeal. She'd never experienced it before, not at close range. On a movie screen, or even on TV, it was nowhere near as potent.

No wonder every woman in the room, regardless of age, was looking at him like a kid through a candy-store window. When he finally got through making the rounds and came back to ask her to dance, she was going to have to work hard to hang onto her composure, or else she'd never be able to look him in the eye again on Monday morning.

But mercy, her palms were sweating just thinking about her right hand in his left, his right hand on her waist.

Pansy and Bianca, along with half a dozen other younger women, waited for him to finish his rounds before engulfing him like a swarm of butterflies. One of them, a pretty redhead, dragged him onto the floor. From her vantage point across the ballroom Callie caught glimpses of him now and then, each time with a different woman.

Hey, I'm over here, remember me? Didn't you ever hear that cliché about dancing with the one that brung you?

She was beginning to see why her aunt thought he needed someone to run interference for him. A few of those women looked as if they were salivating.

Callie glanced at her watch. She slipped her feet out of her shoes, savoring the feel of the cool parquet floor on the soles of her feet. How long was she supposed to wait? She was hungry, but hadn't dared grab something to eat off one of the trays for fear Hank would come back and catch her with her mouth full of crackers piled high with cream cheese and that black glop, whatever it was. It looked like blueberry jam that had sat out too long.

She had to go to the bathroom, too, but she wasn't sure where the one downstairs was located, or if they even had a ladies' room.

Well, of course they did. Manie had showed her the ladies' parlor, where females were allowed to socialize as long as they didn't intrude on the regular members. Manie said Old Tex would roll over in his grave. Callie wondered if the feminist movement had made it as far as West Texas. So far she hadn't seen any signs of it in Royal.

As soon as they'd come downstairs Hank had steered her to a table for two, removed two glasses of champagne from the tray of a passing waiter. He'd just turned to place them on the table when the waiter, obviously young and inexperienced, had backed into a stout gentleman with a walrus mustache and dropped his tray with a tremendous crash, scattering glasses and wine all over the floor.

Everyone had jumped. A woman in pink at the next table

had actually screamed. The poor petrified waiter plainly expected to be fired, if not shot. Callie had risen, intending to go find someone to clean up the wreckage, but things had evolved too quickly. A word here, a nod there, and before she quite realized what he'd done, much less how he'd done it, Hank had the man with the overgrown hedge laughing. The poor petrified waiter no longer looked as if he was about to be sick, and the mess on the floor disappeared as if by magic. For the life of her, she didn't see how he'd accomplished it.

She'd opened her mouth to tell him so, but instead of rejoining her, Hank had gone on talking to the boy. Callie had gawked, hardly believing her eyes, as he lifted a heavy silver tray full of glasses from the hands of another passing waiter and held it over his head, tilting it first one way and then the other without spilling a drop. Then he handed the loaded tray back to the older waiter, patted the younger one on the shoulder and disappeared into the crowd, leaving Callie alone at the table.

That had been ages ago. What in the world was she supposed to be doing? Mingling? Taking notes? Watching to see that no one stole the antique firearms from the glass-front cases on the wall outside the ballroom?

It wasn't a real date. He'd made sure she understood that, right from the first. Still, she'd expected a courtesy dance, even though she'd warned him right up front that she wasn't a good dancer. This was plain old, flat-out desertion.

Maybe she could sue him for desertion and get enough money to rewire the house and buy a minivan and a trailer to move her aunt back to North Carolina.

The band was playing "Yellow Rose of Texas." She recognized it from her mother's old record collection. She hummed along, fingering the skirt of her yellow dress while she thought about what she could take with her tomorrow when she went to visit her aunt.

She yawned, then glanced around, hoping no one saw her. An older brunette in pink seated alone at the next table gave her a commiserating look.

The table on the other side was also occupied by a lone young woman who looked almost as out of place as Callie was feeling. Their gazes caught, and the other woman tendered a shy smile.

"Are you from out of town, too?" Callie leaned closer in order to make herself heard over the noise.

"Goodness, no. I've lived here all my life."

"I'm new in town. Is this—do these people always whoop and holler and carry on like this when they're having fun?"

"I'm no expert. I don't usually go to these affairs, but this year I got roped in because I'm the librarian at the local library. Assistant librarian, actually, but my boss has the flu. We're hoping to get a grant from the money raised tonight."

It was too noisy to converse, but Callie instinctively liked the woman who said her name was Susan Wilkins. "I'm Callie Riley," she yelled over a clashing of cymbals. "Miss Manie—"

And then a young couple jumped up on the bandstand, grabbed the microphone and made what sounded like an announcement. An engagement announcement? With all the hooting, hollering, stomping and whistling, she couldn't be sure. It might've been a yard sale. Somehow, this wasn't the way she'd pictured a fancy ball.

Callie gave up trying to converse. The brunette at the table on her right, whose gown was almost as unsuitable as her own, caught her eye and shrugged. Callie told herself at least she wasn't the only wallflower present. Misery liked company, but there was scant comfort in being stuck on the sidelines, ignored, painfully aware that she didn't belong there and even more painfully aware that everyone else knew it, too.

If only she hadn't lost her common sense somewhere between here and Yakdin County she could have been back at Aunt Manie's house in her pajamas, eating ice cream and watching a rerun of *Diagnosis Murder*.

And darn it, it still wasn't too late. She was on her feet, ready to go collect her things and slip away, when she saw Hank headed her way. Still standing, she looked around uncertainly, wondering if she should get him another glass of champagne to replace the one he'd left on the table, which had to be warm and flat by now.

A smile already forming, she jammed her feet into her shoes in case he asked her to dance. And then she saw him pause at the next table. He said something to the woman in pink, held out his hand, and the two of them merged onto the dance floor without even glancing in Callie's direction.

Well...shoot. Half standing, half crouching, she watched her Prince Not-So-Charming waltz off with the Cinderella in hot pink, then dropped back into her chair, torn between relief and disappointment. Impulsively she downed the glass of champagne she had yet to touch, because she never drank alcohol. And then, in a fit of rebellion, she downed the other glass as well, and waited for Armageddon.

Nothing happened except that she belched. Covering her mouth, she glanced around to see if the assistant librarian named Susan had noticed.

She hadn't, all her attention being focused on a handsome, gray-eyed gentleman who was making his way toward what Callie had come to think of as the wallflower garden.

She belched again and moisture filmed her entire body. Imported champagne evidently packed a potent punch. Her eyes felt as if they were crossed.

"Excuse me, would you care to dance?"

She glanced up too quickly, which made her head reel. "Who, me?" Which was gauche, even for her.

"You're Hank's date, aren't you?"

She shook her head, then took a deep breath to steady herself and said with all the dignity of a drunken undertaker, "You're mistaken. Mr. Langley is my employer. I'm here in the casapity—that is, the capacity—of an, er—um…"

"Guest," the man put in smoothly. He led her out onto the dance floor. Too bemused to resist, Callie followed him. Her feet felt numb. It couldn't be the two glasses of champagne, even though she hadn't eaten since breakfast. Alcohol didn't work that quickly, did it?

"We haven't been introduced, but I'm Sterling Churchill, a friend of Hank's."

"Oh. I'm—"

"Callie. Miss Manie's also a good friend of mine."

There were roughly a hundred questions Callie wanted to ask, but with her tongue feeling almost as numb as her feet, she didn't dare. Instead she contented herself to drift around the crowded dance floor in the arms of a handsome stranger.

He was a wonderful dancer. So smooth, in fact, that she floated along without once thinking about her feet, which she couldn't feel, anyway. And she'd thought she couldn't dance?

Mercy, she was good, she was really good. If Hank ever got around to asking her out onto the floor, she'd just show him a thing or two. She hoped he was watching her.

Leaning back, she studied the face of the attractive

stranger who was gazing over her head as if he were a million miles away. He looked so sad. Bitter? No, sad, she decided, and then with a recklessness that was totally unlike her, she blurted out the first thing that came to mind.

"Why are you so sad?"

He missed a beat. "Why am I what?"

"Sad. Sort of deep-down, where it only shows in your eyes. Has something tragic happened? I know it's none of my business, but if there's anything I can do, I'm real good with people. All us Rileys are like that." She frowned. "Well, not all, but I could talk to her if it's a woman, and when it's a man, it usually is. Does that make sense?"

He shook his head. "No, it doesn't, but don't let it bother you."

"Is it?"

"Is it what?"

"A woman."

He gave a sigh that hinted more of exasperation than of sadness. "Look, my wife left me, we're divorced, there's no other woman in my life because I neither need nor want a woman in my life. Does that satisfy you?"

Fortunately the music ended before she could disgrace herself any further. "I'm sorry," she whispered. "I think I might be a teensy bit drunk."

Her mysterious partner grunted and led her back to the table, leaving her to wonder if she could sneak out of town before she disgraced herself any further.

Maybe if she'd splurged on a pair of glass slippers instead of wearing her tan pumps, hoping they wouldn't show, she could've got through the evening without shaming the entire Riley clan.

Susan had left. She glanced at the brunette in pink, who leaned toward her and whispered loudly, "God, I hate being a charity case, don't you?"

"Is that what we are?" Callie, in a slightly befuddled bit of reasoning, was trying hard to convince herself that she was here in an official capacity, to do whatever it was secretaries did under these circumstances. And even if she didn't take a single note, she was pretty sure she wasn't a charity case.

The two men came together in an alcove at the far end of the ballroom, where the air was fresher and even marginally cooler. "Where'd you go?" Hank asked Sterling Churchill, a friend of long-standing.

"Danced with your lady. I thought that's where you were headed."

"I was, but I saw Tooley's wife and thought I'd pay my respects."

"Another mercy mission?"

"Yeah, I guess. She'd be a damned sight better off if she'd dump that turkey, but some women don't know when they're well off."

"You really set the cat among the pigeons with your new lady. She's not your usual type, man."

"She's not my lady, I don't have a usual type and yeah, I heard a few things, too. Why do you think I've gone out of my way all night to draw off enemy fire?"

"I wouldn't leave her unguarded too much longer, if I were you. She's been hitting the bottle pretty hard."

"Callie? No way."

"Are you tied up after this shindig is over? Because Greg's lined up a meeting with Forrest to go over logistics. Blake's still out of touch, but Greg says he's with us all the way."

"It's going to be late," Hank warned. He glanced at his watch.

"Early's more like it. Might as well get into training.

Feels pretty damn good to be going on a mission again after so many years, doesn't it?''

Hank knew what he meant. "Yeah, it does. I just hope we haven't lost the edge."

After arranging to meet later, he made his way at a leisurely pace across the room, pausing to speak to the women who intercepted him, but moving on again after a few words. He honestly hadn't intended to leave Callie on her own this long, but in a roomful of several hundred people, most of whom he'd known all his life, it was hard to take two steps without being stopped. By the time he heard the rumors and speculation running through the younger set, he figured his best bet was to keep a low profile and deflect attention where Callie was concerned.

Hitting the hard stuff?

Churchill had to be crazy. If she'd had a drinking problem, Manie would have mentioned it. She probably needed some fresh air. So did he, come to think of it. He was getting so he dreaded those things more every year. Maybe he'd break with tradition next year and do something different to raise money for charity, such as a rodeo. Maybe a horse race.

Hell, why not bring in a three-ring circus, it couldn't be any more of a rat race than the annual Cattleman's Club Ball.

Pausing beside a table, he looked around, puzzled. He could've sworn this was where he'd left her.

"Callie?" He glanced around. She was gone. He didn't take the remark about her drinking seriously. Not Callie. Not Miss Manie's little girl, no way. She was probably dancing. Having herself a ball, he hoped, feeling a slight twinge of guilt.

He took the time to survey the dance floor. Not seeing her there, he hurried upstairs, half expecting to find her curled up in one of the wing chairs. She wasn't there, either. Her sweater and purse were gone from the closet, but there was a scrap of paper placed neatly on Manie's desk, anchored with a glass paperweight.

"Thank you for a lovely evening. I called a cab. I'll see you on Monday morning."

Was she being sarcastic?

The truth was, he couldn't be sure. For all she looked so straightforward, he was beginning to think there was more to Callie Riley than met the eye.

Lowering himself into one of the chintz-covered chairs, he absently stroked his throbbing leg. He'd danced more tonight than he had all year, and not once with the lady he'd brought to the ball.

Flowers. He'd send her a floral apology tomorrow, he promised himself, and then remembered that that was the sort of thing Manie had always done for him. He could hardly ask the girl to send herself a bouquet.

Five

He couldn't believe he was doing this. With less than three hours sleep last night, and with a schedule that would floor an ox, Henry Harrison Langley, III, was waiting, hat in hand so to speak, for a twenty-two-year-old woman to finish watering her plants on a Sunday morning at half past nine.

"I'm sorry it took so long, but Aunt Manie has a different set of instructions for each side of the house, and she's bound to ask if I watered this morning."

"You watered so you wouldn't have to lie about it?"

"I watered because I said I would."

"And you always keep your promises." It was a statement, not a question. He'd called first thing this morning to be sure she didn't sneak out of town without him. She'd been frying chicken when he called.

"You don't have to do this, you know."

"I know. Your mature car would get you there just as

well, but you see, I've got this thing about looking out for the health and welfare of my employees."

"I'm only a temporary. Temps don't count."

"I was talking about Manie. What's all this stuff by the door? Does it all go?" He indicated a napkin-covered basket and paper sack with a familiar looking bottle neck sticking out.

"That's a bottle of wine from last night. Mouse said I could take one. Aunt Manie likes sweet wines, but we thought since she had to miss the party, she might like to share some champagne with her friend."

"So you got to meet this friend of hers?"

"No, actually I didn't. Aunt Manie said Marion had a meeting and so she sent her driver instead. It was a real comfortable-looking car, and the driver knew Aunt Manie—he was real sweet about helping her with her suitcase and all, so I guess it's all right."

"Hmm. And the basket?"

"I told you I fried a chicken. Aunt Manie likes it done real crisp and dark brown, and you can't get it like that most places. I got up early so I could make German potato salad, too."

They had fried chicken and potato salad in Texas. Best in the world. But gazing at her earnest little face behind the big, plastic-rimmed glasses, Hank gave up without hoisting the Lone Star flag again. "Listen, Callie, I'm sorry about last night. It was a lousy thing to do, to go off and leave you all alone like that. I can't even offer a decent excuse."

"That's all right, I didn't expect you to stay with me. I was there in a sort of—well, I guess you could call it an official capacity. I knew that."

"A command performance, in other words." On an impulse he didn't even try to understand—nor to resist—he reached up and removed her glasses. She blinked several times but didn't look away, and he thought about how very young she was, and how vulnerable. And how much he was beginning to wish she was neither.

"I met some really nice people. Your friend Mr. Churchill and the assistant librarian." She blinked at him. "Why did you do that?" She didn't back down an inch, just stared right back at him with that oddly mature dignity of hers until he gently replaced her glasses.

Why? He wished to hell he knew. "Ever consider getting contacts?"

"Yes."

He waited. She went on looking him square in the eye. For a lady who appeared to be so direct, he had a growing feeling she was no such thing.

"Are you playing games with me, Callie?"

"No."

He could've sworn she swallowed hard, but that I-shall-not-be-moved look of hers never wavered. He shook his head slowly in reluctant admiration. "Just remember," he said softly, "out here, we play by Texas rules."

"You look like you haven't had a wink of sleep. Why don't you go home and go to bed and let me do this alone? I don't mind."

He nodded soberly, enjoying the internal struggle she was trying so hard not to let show. She'd be a hell of a warrior if guts was all it took. "I'm sure you don't, but I doubt if that clunker of yours would even make it past Windmill Hill."

"I know the way to Midland, my car passed its last inspection with flying colors, and I'm a very safe driver. I've never even had a speeding ticket."

"Why am I not surprised?" Hank murmured, collecting the basket and bottle of warm champagne. He thought fleetingly of all the things he could have accomplished today if he hadn't got hung up on this Quixotic notion that she needed him. By the time he got home, he'd have phone messages and e-mail stacked up like traffic over Dallas-Fort Worth International. He'd be lucky to get to bed again before daybreak.

For the first few miles after they left town, Callie stared out the window, as if fascinated by the oil wells, windmills and the few scrubby mesquites that broke the flat, barren land.

"Not much like North Carolina, is it?" he asked after several minutes of silence had ticked by.

She turned and sent him a look of pleased surprise. "You've been there?"

"Oh, yeah. Blue Ridge Mountains, Outer Banks. A few spots in between." He'd seen at least parts of almost every state in the union. Sometimes he wondered why he'd come back to West Texas. Manie put it down to a bone-deep sense of family obligation, and as she was the only family he had left, he'd let it go at that. Although technically speaking, she wasn't even family.

"Texas is nice, too," Callie said gravely, and he chuckled.

"Yeah, Texas has a lot to be proud of." One of these days before she headed east again, maybe he'd show her around his home state. It was always instructive to see familiar things from a fresh perspective.

He cut a swift look at her profile. Chin up, back straight, eyes front and center. Funny how someone so small and feminine could manage to be both meek and militant at the same time. Idly he wondered just how deep that streak of stubbornness went. And what had caused it.

And what it would take to get beyond it.

Several minutes passed in silence broken only by the purr

of the air conditioner and the whisper of wind whipping over the XJ6. And then she said in that soft, husky, matter-of-fact voice of hers, "May I ask you a personal question? If you don't really want to get married, why are you doing it?"

His hands tightened on the wheel, but he managed to hold it between the lines. "Why am I doing what?"

"You know—Pansy and Bianca. Aunt Manie says you're almost forty years old, and have had women chasing after you since you were knee-high to a grasshopper. She said you've known them both for years, so I guess I just wondered, that's all. About why you waited so long. Not that it's any of my business."

"Right. It's not. Tell me something, do you make a habit of poking your nose where it doesn't belong?"

Thoughtfully she studied her chewed-off thumbnail. "Sometimes. Not if I think it's going to hurt feelings or cause trouble, but you have to admit, it saves a lot of wondering time."

"Wondering time." He turned the concept over in his mind and decided she had a point. "All right, I'll play the game. To save wondering time, why haven't *you* married? Why'd you come all this way to visit a relative you've only met once or twice in your life? What's in it for you?"

"I asked you first."

"Texas rules, remember? Rule number one is ladies first. Come on, Caledonia, you're wasting my valuable wondering time."

She shot him a suspicious look. Taking a deep breath that caused her seat belt to nestle even deeper between her modest breasts, she said, "Well. The answer to your first question is that nobody ever asked me. As for the second one, it's time for Aunt Manie to retire and go back home. She's only a few years younger than Grandpop was."

"Manie? Retire? Never happen."

"She promised to think about it if I filled in for her while she had her operation. Maybe not retiring, but going back with me for a long visit, which is practically the same thing. I'm pretty sure that once I get her home, she'll want to stay."

"Honey, Manie's whole life is right here in Royal. She's been here since before I was even born. She owns a house here."

"It doesn't have a very big yard. My house sits on seven acres, with a real nice garden in the backyard. Aunt Manie loves gardening."

"So I'll buy her a few acres and irrigate it."

"She's long past retirement age."

"She could've retired anytime in the past ten years if she'd wanted to."

Callie shrugged. "She didn't know about me ten years ago. She hadn't been back home in ages and ages, so maybe she'd just sort of given up hope. But we're family, even if there aren't many of us left. Family takes care of family. Grandpop always said families were the building blocks of civilization."

Hank couldn't believe the two of them were fighting about one tiny, tyrannical woman. Couldn't believe he was fighting, period. It wasn't his style. He was in the habit of reaching a decision, stating his position and letting the chips fly. It was one of the perks of wealth and position.

He had a feeling neither commodity cut much ice with Callie.

As they were getting into Midland, Hank filed the subject away for future consideration. "You've got the address of her friend?"

"Right here. Her name's Marion Jones, have you ever met her?"

Hank shook his head. He watched as Callie removed a slip of paper from her neatly organized purse. She read off a street address and said, "I talked to Aunt Manie late yesterday afternoon and told her I'd be here sometime before noon. I don't drive as fast as you do, so we're early."

Hank had no trouble finding the address, as it was not far from where his CEO lived. He was somewhat surprised, but it occurred to him that as Manie knew practically everyone he knew, she might well have formed a friendship with the wife of one of his associates.

He switched off the engine and swung open the door, braced for the waves of baking heat that arose from the paved driveway. He was used to it. Callie wasn't. If he remembered correctly, her part of the country was hot, too, but it was a different type of heat. At least it rained occasionally in North Carolina. In West Texas, drought was a fact of life. Rain happened, but so rarely that folks had worn out all the old jokes about Noah's Ark, the forty-day rain and the fact that West Texas got only a couple of inches that year.

The door was opened by a uniformed maid. "Mees Riley?" she said in a heavily accented voice, ignoring Hank to smile at Callie. "Mees Manie is expecting you. She's in the sunroom."

The sunroom? At high noon in August?

"I brought some fried chicken, the way Aunt Manie likes it—oh, and there's potato salad, too. No eggs or mayonnaise, but I guess you'd better put it in the refrigerator anyway, if there's room."

The smiling maid took the basket and the wine and turned away, and Hank thought about the massive stainless-steel refrigerator in his own kitchen that was stocked fresh daily by his kitchen staff.

If there was *room?* Bless her heart, did she think they still used ice boxes out here in the hinterlands?

Manie called out from a room across the large tiled foyer. "I'm out here, you all come on out. Watch the step-down."

Callie was too busy watching the plants. They were everywhere, massive, flowering vines and leathery-leafed plants, orchids of every variety crawling on overhead supports. She would've fallen if Hank hadn't taken her arm.

"Watch it, there might be quicksand bogs," he joked, trying and failing to ignore the feel of her soft warm skin and the subtle fragrance that drifted up from her hair. It wasn't the orchids, nor any of the other exotic flora, it was Callie, pure and simple. He'd noticed it last night.

"Marion had to go to the airport to meet some people. I'm real sorry you all won't get to meet each other. Now, tell me everything. How'd the ball go? Honey, did you get a pretty dress? Did you go to that place I told you about on the corner of Main and Marshall? Were there any engagements announced? I was kind of worried about that new place that supplies temporary workers, but Hanna over at Claire's says they're real reliable. How'd we do for the fund? Did we top last year's total? Are there any—?"

Hank held up a hand. "Whoa. I'll give you all the data, but first I want to know how you're feeling."

"I'm going to be just fine. A tad uncomfortable right now, if you want to know the truth, but they tell me that's normal. I'll be back in fighting trim in no time at all. Now, what about Callie's dress?"

They both answered at once. Callie said it was on sale, Hank said it was yellow and Manie shook her head. "You went right out and bought the cheapest thing in town, didn't you?"

The two women talked about her gown some more, until Hank took pity on Callie and changed the subject. She was blushing. He hadn't known women still blushed. None of the ones he knew did. Or if they did, they wore enough makeup to cover it.

It was nearly two when they left, having devoured the chicken and salad Callie had brought, along with Texas cantaloupes, fresh rolls and iced tea. Manie hadn't urged them to stay, although Hank wanted to meet this Jones woman who'd had a meeting on Thursday and had to meet a party at the airport today. She was beginning to seem a little too elusive to suit him.

But Manie was looking tired, so Rosa, the housekeeper, brought Callie her basket, the napkin folded neatly inside, and showed them out. When Callie mentioned Miss Jones, and how much they appreciated her looking after Miss Riley, the woman looked puzzled. Hank repeated the words in Spanish, but she only smiled, nodded and closed the door.

"Satisfied?" he asked after they'd left the town behind.

"I guess the doctors know what they're doing, sending her home this soon."

"You're supposed to be the expert on matters medical." He was wearing an open-neck shirt. Now he reached up and unfastened another button, adjusting the air vent to allow the frigid air to play over the bronzed skin of his throat.

"No, I'm not. Just because I worked for a doctor and knew all the sales reps and stood in a few times for the nurse, that doesn't mean I'm any expert."

"Do you want a second opinion?"

She thought about it and then shook her head. "I think this friend of hers would call her doctor if there was the least cause for worry, don't you? Anyway, Aunt Manie tends to be independent. She's a lot like Grandpop that way. I thought about it on the drive west, and I decided the best way to convince her to do something—for her own good, of course—is to keep nattering around the edges until she thinks it's all her own idea.''

''Is that what you're doing? Steering her into deciding to go back home with you?''

Callie nodded. ''We've been writing back and forth ever since the funeral. I reminded her that now I had this great big house just going to waste, and how I'd painted it. And about the garden and all. Well, of course, she saw that when she was there. The collards were looking good, but the beans and tomatoes were long past their prime, but that's only temporary.''

''Of course it is,'' he said solemnly, and they sped along for another five miles.

Middle of the afternoon. Hot as hell. Even with the best air conditioner in the world, the psychological effect of all that August sun beating down from a cloudless sky was making him sweat. Something sure was. Callie, too. She'd eased her skirt up over her knees and was fanning herself with a scrap of handkerchief. He tried not to look, he really did, but the battle was lost the minute she'd bared those small, rounded kneecaps and he'd caught a glimpse of silky white thigh.

She fell silent, which was just as well, because he was having trouble concentrating. Was she doing it deliberately? Flashing the flesh, tossing out tantalizing topics and letting them lie there?

Yeah, right. Like beans and tomatoes.

He wanted to get into her mind, simply because he couldn't figure her out.

Unfortunately that wasn't all he wanted to get into.

She's a kid, Langley! She's way out of your league.

He eased the pedal to the floor, wishing he was out on his dirt bike where he could outride his problems for a few hours. Problems such as this marriage business. The fact that his fortieth birthday was rushing toward him like a bat out of hell, and that he was without a wife, without issue as they said in legal circles—and with an estate that grew at an obscene rate in spite of a lack of any real interest on his part. He wasn't cut out to be a millionaire. He'd be a hell of a lot more content doing something—almost anything—on a smaller scale.

"I wouldn't blame her much if she decided not to go."

"Sorry. Did I miss something?"

"Aunt Manie. You saw where she was staying. What if she wants to stay on here in Texas? Grandpop's place is wonderful, but it's nothing like Miss Jones's house. That fancy sunroom and all—I mean, I could probably afford a cold frame, but…" She sighed and began gnawing her lower lip. Hank reached over and laid a comforting hand on hers.

Some comfort. Her hand happened to be on her lap. His fingers brushed her thigh, and he could've sworn sparks flew.

She felt it, too. He could tell by the way she sucked in her breath. In an effort to defuse the tension, he reached out and switched on the radio, then tuned quickly away from the music he'd preset to a weather report.

Pansy called him manipulative. He'd never denied it. Like most men, he preferred getting his way. Over the years he'd gotten pretty damn good at it, but Callie wasn't fair game.

"You know what?" she asked in that soft, husky, made-up-my-mind-about-something voice of hers, "I don't think you're nearly as helpless and vulnerable as Aunt Manie says you are. She'll rest a lot easier when it comes time to leave, though, if you've got a wife to look after you, so I'm going to do my best to hold off the stampede until you make up your mind which one you want. Doc Teeter was seventy-seven years old, and you wouldn't believe the way the women chased after him. They even waited at the office for him, with cakes and invitations to supper and bingo. Sometimes two or three at a time, so you see, I've had practice.''

"Rough duty, huh?'' Either she was even more of an innocent than he'd thought, or she was the slickest little con artist in seven states.

"Worse than that. I think a few of them even thought there might be something between me and Doc, but he was like my grandfather. In fact, he was a friend of my grandfather, which is how I got the job.''

"And now that your doctor's retired, Manie's appointed you my guard dog.'' He had to laugh, picturing these two small Riley women guarding his six-foot-two, one-hundred-eighty-seven-pound body against an army of females in size zilch designer dresses.

"Actually she gave me a whole list of duties, but mostly I'm supposed to act as head referee in the Hank Stakes. She's afraid now that the coast is clear, Pansy and Bianca might move in and arrange to be caught in a compromising situation. You know, the way people did in all those Regency romances?''

Hank cut her a swift glance to see if she was pulling his leg, but there wasn't a glimmer of a smile in her face. "Honey, you're a couple of centuries behind the times. Politicians are about the only ones who can be compromised these days, and even then, one good spin cycle and they're clean as driven snow.''

"Hmm,'' she said thoughtfully. "Well, personally, if you want to know what I think, I think you're old enough to fight your own battles.''

"Do you, Callie?'' he asked, bemused by this small,

plain woman wearing a limp cotton dress that probably cost less than one of his T-shirts.

She nodded emphatically. "However, if there's anything you want to tell me—I mean about which one you want to win, I'll be glad to listen. It's the least I can do."

He couldn't help it, he burst out laughing. By the time he'd sobered enough to notice, she was grinning from ear to ear.

"You little monkey, you do it on purpose, don't you?"

"Do what on purpose?"

"This act of yours. You know you crack me up, sitting there solemn as a judge, going on about how sensitive and vulnerable I am, and how you've vowed to protect me at all costs."

"I didn't say anything about the costs, I only said Aunt Manie thinks—"

"No, she doesn't."

"She said so."

"I hate to tell you this, honey, but your great-aunt is a devious woman. I'm beginning to think it might run in the family."

She was silent for so long, Hank suspected he might be on to something. What the devil was that pair up to? Were they in it together, or was each working toward a separate end?

They'd both bear watching. And watching Caledonia Riley in action was something he was beginning to enjoy a little too much.

As for Callie, she felt his eyes on her more than a few times on the ride back to Royal. She couldn't catch him at it without the risk of being caught herself. All the same, she knew when she was being looked at. The thing she didn't know was why.

He probably didn't trust her. She'd either said too much

or too little. He probably resented the fact that she was here to steal a valuable employee from him, but if he thought Texas rules were something, wait until he came up against Riley rules.

"Hungry?" he asked, dropping back to ten miles above the limit.

"Not really."

"Humor me, I hate to dine alone."

"No, you don't. Manie said you almost never went out for dinner if you could get out of it, and I know you order lunch sent up almost every day."

"So, I happen to like Mouse's cooking."

"Why does everyone call him Mouse?"

"Maybe someday, if you're a good girl, I'll tell you the story." He veered into the parking lot at Claire's. As it was early, even for a Sunday, there were only a handful of cars there.

"I can't go in there," Callie whispered, suddenly conscious of her limp cotton dress and her bare feet in flat sandals. She'd dusted a layer of powder over her freckles before she'd left home this morning, but by now she'd be shining like an oil slick.

"What, you don't like French food? Lucky for you, I happen to know where we can get a couple of really fine chili dogs, with the best coconut pie in the world."

"Maybe you'd better just take me home. You've wasted a whole day, and—"

"I've wasted nothing. Manie's my friend. Believe it or not, she means as much to me as she does to you. You want to know what I think?"

"Not really, but you're going to tell me anyway, aren't you?"

"I think you're jealous because Manie would rather be

here in Texas with me than go back to North Carolina with you."

"I am not—"

"Sure you are. Admit it, Callie. I've got something you want, and you're all bent out of shape about it. Honey, Manie's whole life is right here in Royal. She's lived here a damned sight longer than she ever lived in North Carolina. She's got good friends here who mean a lot to her, and that means that no matter what you want to believe, she doesn't really need you."

"That's not true," she whispered.

"Yeah, it is. Get over it, Callie. Go back home and get started on a family of your own."

She took a deep, bracing breath. If he'd whopped her across the face, it couldn't have hurt any more than his words had, because there was an element of truth in them. "You don't know that," she said with every appearance of composure.

If there was one thing Callie was good at, it was hiding her feelings. Hiding her loneliness. Hiding her fear of being left alone. Lord knows, she'd had enough practice. For as long as she could remember, her parents had fought like cats and dogs. She'd been thirteen years old when her father had come home one day and announced that he'd quit his job. Mama had let out a screech that could be heard all the way into Wilkes County.

Then they'd noticed Callie and tried to pretend they'd just been fooling around, but she'd seen those same sickening false smiles too many times to be fooled. They'd sent her out to play, but before she'd even cleared the front porch she could hear them through the open window, going at it tooth and nail.

"—wasting my life—"

"—tied down—"

"—married too young!"

It had been ugly. Callie had felt like throwing up, but she'd heard it all before. It happened. Daddies ran off, Mamas got lawyers, papers got served and kids got their lives screwed up.

Right then and there, she'd started making plans for the future. On the plus side, she had Grandpop. He chewed tobacco and told the same old stories over and over again, but at least he was always there. Steady, reliable and best of all, he loved her.

The funny part was that her parents, once they got everything out in the open and finished going through what Callie thought of as their change of life, had settled down and got along like a house afire. Which had taught her two ,more of Life's Lessons: Don't try to jam square pegs into round holes because it's a miserable fit, and whenever possible, speak your mind. It saves trouble in the long run.

She also believed in keeping a low profile, as in dressing modestly and not calling attention to herself. She'd read somewhere that to have what we want is riches, but to be able to do without is power. So she'd kept her wants modest, and now here she was, within spitting distance of having them fulfilled.

And no gold-plated, tinhorn cowboy with a bunch of oil wells in his hip pocket was going to keep her from it, Texas rules or not.

"A hot dog would be just lovely. I like onions on mine."

Six

The Royal Diner it was. Callie reached for the one-page, plastic-covered menu. Hank gently removed it from her hand and ordered for her. And then had the pleasure of watching her tackle one of the Royal's famous hot dogs, along with a peach milkshake. By the time she'd wiped the last of the chili off her chin and fingers, he'd already signaled for two slabs of coconut pie, which happened to be his favorite. A few minutes later, Big Lou Macon waddled over with their dessert and leaned up against the bench to ask if he wanted a puppy.

"What kind?" Callie asked.

"Heinz 57," said Lou, about the same time Hank told her definitely not. One thing led to another as the two women started talking pets. From pets they moved on to talk about cousins. Callie had none, but Lou had seventeen, nine of whom owned pets and three of whom were currently in jail for one social gaffe or another.

Hank finished his pie and took a forkful of Callie's while the two women moved on to ailments. Again, Callie had none, but Lou's were legion, and since everyone in town knew about Manie's niece, and that she'd once worked for a physician, it didn't take long for Lou to start pumping.

"You might try tea tree oil," Callie advised. Her glasses had slid down her nose, and Hank reached across the table, removed them and dropped them into his shirt pocket. Ignoring him, she told the waitress earnestly to rub it on her toenail three times a day. "Oh, and take garlic and—"

"That does it." He dug out his wallet, fished out two bills and shoved them under the napkin dispenser. "Goodnight, Lou, come on, Callie, time to go home."

"Oh, but—"

"But nothing," he said firmly, planting a hand on her back to urge her out the door. "You were practicing medicine without a licence. In Texas, that can put you out of circulation."

"But I haven't finished my pie yet," she wailed.

"I'll have Lou send you three pies tomorrow. You can have pie for breakfast, pie for lunch and pie for dinner, all right?"

He almost laughed at the mutinous expression on her face. Silver-blue eyes blazing, splashes of color on both cheeks, not to mention the speck of mustard at the corner of her mouth—damned if she wasn't more tempting than the pie.

He opened the car door and held it while she slid her shapely little rear end onto the seat, then swung both feet inside. Funny, the way he noticed little things like that about her. Most women climbed into a car headfirst, butt last. And while that method had its advantages, particularly for the bystander, he sort of liked the way Callie did it. It was…graceful.

He slid under the steering wheel, reminded her to fasten her belt, and it hit him again. That tantalizing fragrance that sent him back in time to the kitchen at his father's first house, back when his mother had still been alive.

"Well?" He waited. "Aren't you going to chew me out?"

"No."

"I sort of wish you would."

"I know you do."

"Why?"

"Why what?"

He slapped the wheel with the heel of his hand. Dammit, she was doing it to him again. Playing games with his mind, not to mention what she was doing to his libido. Watching her dig into a loaded hot dog, watching the tip of her tongue flick out to take care of the overflow—going on with Lou about dogs and toenails, while he sat there, randy as a goat, he'd had to wonder why he'd ever thought he knew something about women.

Now she was fooling around with his mind. For a lady who claimed to be such a straight shooter, she was remarkably devious. To make matters worse, she was Manie's niece. Manie would scalp him if he so much as laid a finger on her. Hell, he'd even hand her the knife.

"Thank you for supper. I'm sorry if I upset you. I didn't mean to, I was only trying to be helpful."

She was sorry if she'd upset him. Like he didn't have his future all mapped out before she'd showed up and started drawing crazy lines all over his nice, neat map. "I know you were, honey."

Did she do it deliberately? Turn him on, only to put him

on the defensive? Entire boards of directors had been known to quail at the lift of one of his eyebrows. A minor part of his survival training when he'd applied to join Special Forces had been a blindfolded three-meter drop into deep water, wearing cap, fatigues, boots, pistol belt, first-aid pouch, two full canteens, two ammo pouches, harness and rifle. He'd had to surface and swim to safety, removing only the blindfold.

Compared to dealing with Callie Riley, it was a piece of cake.

Cruising through town to the neat, middle-class neighborhood where Manie lived, he tried to figure out how she did it, and whether or not it was deliberate. Everything about her was understated. She didn't do anything to call attention to herself, which made him all the more curious. When a situation started to bug him, he generally took it apart, analyzed the components, pinpointed the problem and did something about it. The one thing he never did was waste time brooding.

One of these days he was going to get inside her head and discover who was hiding behind that Little Miss Muffet mask.

"Hold on," he said when she started to climb out. He went around and opened the car door, watched her knees swing around, her small, sandal-shod feet hit the ground, and then he walked her to the door of Manie's house, took her key and unlocked it.

"Thank you for—"

"I'll look around to be sure everything's all right," he told her, just as if they lived in a high crime area instead of a town where half the citizens didn't even bother to lock their doors.

He made a cursory walk-though while she waited in the

front hall, then she thanked him again and held out her hand. Like a blooming idiot, he shook it, thinking about the way Pansy had launched herself at him a few nights ago and kissed the living daylights out of him. He was half tempted to—

No, he wasn't.

"My glasses?"

"What glasses? Oh, yeah—these." *Smooth, man, real smooth.*

Hank wasn't used to feeling like a jerk. The fact that the woman who was doing it to him was none other than little Miss What-you-see-is-what-you-get Riley didn't help much. Hank liked women as much as the next man. Liked to think he understood them, or at least as well as any man could ever understand any woman. Most of the ones he knew socially were as predictable as the weather around these parts. Hot, dry and windy.

Callie was cool and calm. She could go for hours without saying a word and then come out with the damnedest things. He thought about that cliché about still waters and figured he'd better leave before he did anything he'd regret. Muttering about an early night, he fled.

Up early the next morning after another restless night, Hank forced himself to concentrate on the latest batch of P&E statements. At nine, on his third cup of black coffee, he swung around to face the window, hoisted his boots to the windowsill and placed a call to his broker concerning a small, innovative software company that was about to go public.

"Oscar, you know that outfit we talked about last week? I want it. See what you can do about it and get back to me." He hung up, wondering what old Tex would have thought of the changes that had taken place over the course of three generations. With the feds trying to hog-tie the players with regulations, the silicon trade these days reminded him of the wildcat days here in Royal, back when Tex Langley had brought in his first handful of wells.

Ten past nine. He'd scheduled a meeting in San Diego for later in the day. With a two-day backlog of work to plow through first, he couldn't seem to concentrate. Making a deliberate effort, he focused on the Pacific Rim investment group he'd be meeting in a matter of hours, only to drift off into another nonproductive daydream.

"Crap," he muttered. He poured himself another cup of coffee, downed it and rubbed his gut, then opened another folder and stared out the window, the refrain from an old blues number tugging at his memory.

New Orleans. A place on Bourbon Street—a few guys from Special Ops blowing off steam. Slap-bass player with a patch over one eye. Blues singer with a beat-up guitar and a voice like a cement mixer belting out a song about a woman named Caledonia.

"Cal'donia, Cal'donia..." There was something about her hard head or her big feet, he couldn't remember which. Grinning, he was grabbing a fistful of air, growling a heartfelt, "Yeah!" when the door opened and Callie said, "Did you call me? I was on the phone and I thought I heard..."

The chair swiveled around. Papers slid from the folder on his lap, and he started to chuckle. Being caught acting the fool wasn't something that happened to him often, probably not often enough. "Tell me something, Callie, did you ever find yourself so far up a twisted creek you couldn't find your way back again?"

Gravely she thought it over, and then she asked, "Is that a rhetorical question?"

"I'm not sure." His thoughtful gaze took in the way her tan skirt accentuated a narrow waist and small, nicely rounded hips. For a man who'd always appreciated subtlety, he'd come dangerously close to overlooking her.

Now he just wished to hell he could.

"Well, if you really want to know, when I get all muddled up about something, I usually sleep on it. I think my subconscious mind must see a lot of things my conscious mind misses, because as often as not when I wake up, the answers are all laid out on my pillow, plain as day. Does that help?"

She looked so worried he wanted to gather her up in his arms and comfort her. "Thanks, it helps a whole lot." So now he'd go to bed thinking about Callie lying there in her maidenly bed, waiting diligently for her subconscious to come up with the orders of the day.

Oh, yeah. Big help.

"Anytime, sir."

"Anytime, *what?*" His voice was dangerously soft.

One hand on the door, she grinned over her shoulder. "Hank. Oh, and Hank, do you mind if I leave for lunch a few minutes early? I thought I'd stop by the library and pick up a mystery. All Aunt Manie has is gardening books, and there's nothing much on TV this week."

"Sure, take as long as you need."

After she left, he downed three aspirin, chased them with a pint of milk, then settled down at his desk again. He still had the day's mail to go though before he left town. She'd sorted it into neat stacks, the way Manie had showed her. Most of the stuff was dealt with at headquarters, his input done electronically. Even so, he got about fifteen pounds a day of periodicals, solicitations, legitimate business, per-

WELCOME TO THE
CASINO!
Try your luck at the Roulette Wheel ...
Play a hand of Twenty-One!

How to play:

1. Play the Roulette and Twenty-One scratch-off games, as instructed on the opposite page, to see that you are eligible for FREE BOOKS and a FREE GIFT!

2. Send back the card and you'll receive TWO brand-new Silhouette Desire® novels. These books have a cover price of $3.75 each in the U.S. and $4.25 each in Canada, but they are yours to keep absolutely free.

3. There's no catch. You're under no obligation to buy anything. We charge nothing — ZERO — for your first shipment. And you don't have to make any minimum number of purchases — not even one!

4. The fact is, thousands of readers enjoy receiving books by mail from the Silhouette Reader Service™ before they're available in stores. They like the convenience of home delivery, and they love our discount prices!

5. We hope that after receiving your free books you'll want to remain a subscriber. But the choice is yours — to continue or cancel, any time at all!

So why not take us up on our invitation, with no risk of any kind. You'll be glad you did!

Play Twenty-One For This Exquisite Free Gift!

THIS SURPRISE
MYSTERY GIFT
WILL BE YOURS
FREE WHEN YOU PLAY
TWENTY-ONE

It's fun, and we're giving away *FREE GIFTS* to all players!

PLAY ROULETTE!

Scratch the silver to see that the ball has landed on 7 RED, making you eligible for TWO FREE romance novels!

PLAY TWENTY-ONE!

Scratch the silver to reveal a winning hand! Congratulations, you have Twenty-One. Return this card promptly and you'll receive a fabulous free mystery gift, along with your free books!

YES!

Please send me all the free Silhouette Desire® books and the gift for which I qualify! I understand that I am under no obligation to purchase any books, as explained on the back of this card.

Name: _____
(PLEASE PRINT)

Address: _____ Apt.#: _____

City: _____ State: _____ Zip: _____

The Silhouette Reader Service™ — Here's how it works:

Accepting your 2 free books and mystery gift places you under no obligation to buy anything. You may keep the books and gift and return the shipping statement marked "cancel." If you do not cancel, about a month later we'll send you 6 additional novels and bill you just $3.12 each in the U.S., or $3.49 each in Canada, plus 25¢ delivery per book and applicable taxes if any.* That's the complete price and — compared to the cover price of $3.75 in the U.S. and $4.25 in Canada — it's quite a bargain! You may cancel at any time, but if you choose to continue, every month we'll send you 6 more books, which you may either purchase at the discount price or return to us and cancel your subscription.

*Terms and prices subject to change without notice. Sales tax applicable in N.Y. Canadian residents will be charged applicable provincial taxes and GST.

If offer card is missing write to: Silhouette Reader Service, 3010 Walden Ave., P.O. Box 1867, Buffalo, NY 14240-9952

BUSINESS REPLY MAIL
FIRST-CLASS MAIL   PERMIT NO 717   BUFFALO NY

POSTAGE WILL BE PAID BY ADDRESSEE

SILHOUETTE READER SERVICE
3010 WALDEN AVE
PO BOX 1867
BUFFALO NY 14240-9952

NO POSTAGE
NECESSARY
IF MAILED
IN THE
UNITED STATES

sonal mail and unpersonal mail that was marked personal to get his attention.

There was a birthday card from his insurance agent, a reminder, as if he needed it, that no man, no matter how lofty his position, controlled every aspect of his own life. Hell, he couldn't even control his own love life. With two of the most beautiful, eligible women in the world on his short list, his attention kept straying over to the other side of the pasture.

She barely even had breasts, for cripes sake. Never mind that Bianca's cleavage was mostly silicon valley. Never mind that Pansy thought kids were, in her own words, icky. Both women were the right age, moved comfortably in the right circles and were experienced enough to know what marriage was all about.

Callie didn't know scat. He wouldn't be surprised if she crawled into her virginal bed wearing white cotton drawers under a flannel nightgown. So how come all he had to do was look at that fresh, dewy face, those big, guileless eyes to start thinking about rumpled sheets, soft, shared laughter, and the heady scent of sex?

Was it all part of some devious game she was playing? Trying to lure him into dropping his guard so she could spring her trap? Manie had probably told her all about him. Manie thought he'd hung the moon, not that she cut him much slack when she thought he was getting too big for his britches.

What if Callie had seen her chance to land herself a trophy husband and jumped at it? It wouldn't be the first time he'd had to deal with that sort of thing. Groupies were a fact of life for men in his position. He'd always gently but firmly declined their offers, but this time it might not be so easy.

Callie was still out to lunch when Greg stopped by. Gregory Hunt was one of a very few men who had access to Hank's inner sanctum.

"Been hitting the French Roast again, huh?"

"You're worse than Manie. Can't a guy have a few cups of coffee without being hauled up before the D.A.?"

"Better than being hauled up before the M.D. The stuff eats a hole in your gut, man. Take the cure."

"Laying off coffee's not going to ease the pain in this case."

"Want to talk about it?"

"Not particularly."

Greg shrugged. "Your call. Hey, I saw your new secretary on her way into the library. Interesting type."

"Not really. She's Manie's great-niece, that's all."

"Right."

"Are you implying something?"

"What's to imply?"

Hank scowled. As an experienced lawyer, Greg Hunt was an expert when it came to sizing up potential witnesses and jurors. He had a sharp eye for the kind of detail most men missed. He was stalling now, beating around the bush, but two could play that game. "So tell me, what do you make of her?"

Greg steepled his fingers. "Who, Little Bo Peep?"

Hank smothered a grin. He'd thought of her as Little Miss Muffet, but then, what the devil did either of them know about nursery rhymes?

"She's younger than most of the ones you're interested in."

"What makes you think I'm interested?"

"You asked me. I'm telling you. As for the rest, I'd say she's Bible Belt, a lot smarter than she looks, pretty inexperienced sexually—possibly even a virgin. In other words, look but don't touch, man. She's way out of your league.''

"Besides, Manie would kill me.''

"You got it.''

Greg's face turned more serious. "Blake's in.'' Blake was Greg's younger brother, a wealthy young playboy who also happened to excel at undercover work for the government. "He's been out of the country for the past few months, but I managed to get through to him last night.''

"These kids you mentioned. How old are they?''

"The twins? Let's see, Anna's boy is four, the twins are only a few months old. The kids make it doubly complicated, but we can't leave them behind. Anna promised her late sister. She's not the kind of woman to go back on her word.''

"You seem to know her pretty damned well considering it's been four years, and you were together only a few months.''

Shutters came down over Greg's clear blue eyes. Hank took the hint and backed off. "I'll have Pete stand by with the Avenger.''

"We'll need to wait until Blake gets into town.''

"Right. Meanwhile, I'll have a special safe line installed here at the clubhouse and line up a few encrypted handsets.''

"I owe you, man.'' Indicating that the discussion was ended, Greg mentioned an old Marine Corps buddy he'd seen on the news recently, which brought on a few more stories of their respective military days.

Both men came from old money, well tended. Both men had joined the military largely as a gesture of rebellion. The fires had since burned low, but Hank wanted to believe the coals were still there, well banked and ready to flare up again if the occasion demanded.

"Did it ever occur to you that what you're fighting is part of the aging-boomer syndrome?" Greg asked. "That dirt bike of yours—man, that's high school stuff. And this grizzly bear mood you've been in lately."

"You trying to tell me you never race your engines, rev 'em up to full thrust just to hear the roar of power, to prove you've still got what it takes?" Hank asked with a quizzical look.

"Not out in public, the way you do." He chuckled. "Ever consider the fact that you might be a throwback to the early wildcatting days? I hear old Tex was hell on wheels in his day."

"Yeah, I've considered it."

He also considered the fact that Greg had jumped on this rescue mission without a second thought and that every last one of them had piled on with him.

Maybe they weren't as far over the hill as he'd been thinking. "I'm flying up to San Diego this afternoon. Join me?"

"I'm expecting another call from Blake." The younger man rose to go. "How's the Avenger doing for you, anyway?" Greg's family owned the company that designed and built the luxury jet.

"All it lacks is a hot tub."

"I'll pass it on."

"Seriously, I'll have Pete on standby as soon as you give the word."

Greg left then, and Hank shoved aside the file folder, turned to his computer and typed in a command. With narrowed eyes he scanned the rows of numbers, called up two more files and then gave it up. Not quite forty damn years old, and already his powers of concentration had started to atrophy.

Callie. Was it the challenge that turned him on, the lure of the forbidden? The fact that she was strictly off limits?

Or the fact that she was obviously not impressed by either his Swiss account or his manly charms?

Callie found the Royal Public Library with no trouble at all. It was in the government center, smack in the middle of town, no more than a block and a half from the club. She walked in on story-time. One small adult surrounded by a swarm of children under the age of six. She'd been hoping to find the assistant librarian alone. Even though she'd soon be heading back to Carolina, it would be nice to have a friend here, and Susan had struck her at the ball as someone she would like to get to know.

Their eyes met now over two rows of small bodies in small chairs, and Callie detected a silent plea.

"Children," said the slender, attractive redhead, "We'll have a time-out now, and when we come back, there'll be lemonade and cookies for everyone who remembers how we behave in a library."

They were no wilder than the average group of that age after being told to be quiet. Callie watched, amused, as they scattered like a covey of quail, whispering, giggling and fighting over whose turn it was to pass around the cookies.

"How do you manage alone?" she asked.

"Usually I don't. The head librarian's still out, my volunteer didn't show up and I woke up with a sinus headache."

"In case you didn't hear me over the noise of the ball, I'm Callie Riley. You might know my aunt, Romania Riley? Shall I herd a few to the bathroom for you? Believe me, I know the drill.''

"That's right, you used to work for a doctor, didn't you? Would you mind? We go in shifts, three at a time. If they take too long, remind them of the cookies.''

By the time the parents began to show up to collect their offspring, Callie felt as if she'd known Susan Wilkins for years. Once the last child left, she lent a hand to setting the place to rights, shelving books, brushing up crumbs and wiping up spills.

"How does it feel to know you're the envy of half the women in Royal?'' Susan asked once the children's corner was in order again.

"Who, me? You mean they all want to be secretaries?''

"They all want to be Mrs. H. H. Langley, III. Manie's been guarding the gates for years, afraid her precious Hank will get his heart cracked.''

"You think that's likely?'' Callie picked up a rumpled hair ribbon, laid it on the desk, her eyes lingering on the return address of an unopened envelope there. Buddy's Sperm Bank Clinic?

That had to be a joke.

Susan was saying, "It's hard to tell about Mr. Langely. He's always been one of those larger-than-life men nobody really knows much about. You hear rumors, though. Did you know he has this great big old motorcycle that he races all over the countryside? Does that sound like the kind of thing you'd expect a man in his position to do?''

"He's the only man in his position I've ever known, so I'm no authority.''

Buddy's Sperm Bank Clinic?

"Well, take it from me, there are a lot of rich men around these parts, but I don't know of another one who puts on a pair of ragged, faded blue jeans, old boots and a black T-shirt that fits him like a coat of paint and goes roaring off across country like a member of that heck's angels gang or something.''

Callie's imagination instantly shifted into overdrive. Lordy, the man was enough to contend with in those form-fitting jeans and body-hugging Western shirts. Torn jeans? The mind boggled.

She selected three mysteries, placed them on the desk as far away from the intriguing envelope as she could and dug out her driver's license. ''Do you think I could get some kind of a temporary card?''

''Put that thing away, you don't need any card. We all know Miss Manie, and besides, if you forget to turn in your books before you go back to North Carolina, your boss will take care of it. He's already endowed half the town. A few books won't break him.''

Fifty miles to the north, Manie and Marion Jones watched the Astros play Atlanta while they sipped their drinks. Gin and tonic for Marion. Iced blackberry wine for Manie. Marion, naturally, was an Astros fan, while Manie, for obscure reasons of her own, rooted for the Braves.

Marion dipped manicured fingers into the bowl of popcorn on the antique Italian table between their two chairs. ''Have you told her yet?''

''I'm waiting for the right—oh, shoot! Did you see that pitch? It was a mile off the plate! Get with it, Maddux!''

''You're not doing her any favors, letting her go on hoping this way.''

''We'll see, we'll see,'' said Manie, an enigmatic smile carving deep creases in her weathered cheeks.

The Braves won, 3 to 0. Marion shoved a five-dollar bill

across the table. Manie took it and tucked it in the pocket of her mulberry silk robe. "I told you so," she said smugly.

"One of these days, lady…"

"Humph."

Hank was on the phone when Callie got back, carrying her lunch in a paper bag. His door was open, his feet propped on the broad windowsill. It was his thinking position, according to Aunt Manie. When he had a problem, he put his feet up and stared out the window.

"Callie, come in here a minute, will you?"

She swallowed a French fry, shoved the grease-stained sack behind the fax machine, wiped her fingers and adjusted her dutiful smile. "Yes, sir?"

"I thought we'd dealt with that."

"Dealt with what?"

"That 'sir' business."

She wasn't about to tell him that she needed every advantage she could beg, borrow or steal to keep him in his place. Formality wasn't much of a defense, but it was all she had.

"Discipline makes for efficiency, sir," she told him solemnly. *Henry Harrison Langley, III on a motorcycle? Wearing tight, faded jeans and a skintight T-shirt?*

"If I want efficiency, I'll have someone sent down from Midland. Now cut the crap and look at these paint samples. I'm thinking of having Manie's house repainted while she's gone, and I want to put in the order before I leave for San Diego. What do you think, cool white? Antique white? Caribbean white? Damned if I can see any difference."

"You're thinking of *what?*"

"Painting Manie's house. You know, that stuff you

smear around when you want to change the color or prevent weathering?''

"I know what paint is. What I don't know is why you want to paint Aunt Manie's house. It looks fine to me.''

"Sun's hard on paint. Let it go too long, and the stuff starts peeling, and then it has to be sandblasted.''

"Everything in Texas is sandblasted every day.''

"Not always. It's just a little breezier than usual for this time of the year.''

"If you want my opinion, I think her house is just fine the way it is. If she sells it, the new owner might want to paint it some other color.''

"Why the devil would she sell it?'' Hank was seated, Callie was standing as far away as she could and still look at the paint strips. It amused him to invade her personal space only because he knew it bothered her. It was a bully's trick. She was surprised that he would resort to it. She dealt with it by trying hard to ignore the heat of his body, the scent of his shaving lotion, or whatever it was that made him smell masculine and sexy and clean and dangerous.

Whatever it was, it ought to be against the law.

"People sell houses all the time,'' she said, adopting the tone she used to reason with difficult patients. "Either they get transferred or the children leave home and they don't need as much space. Or maybe they retire and go to live with relatives because they need the security of having someone close by who loves them and will look after them.''

She waited for his reaction, torn between telling him everything about her plans and telling him nothing. He already knew far too much.

"Yeah, well...decide on a color while I'm gone, will you? Meanwhile, call downstairs and have my car brought around. Chances are I'll be back sometime tonight, so go ahead and set up tomorrow's appointments, starting at nine. You know the drill. Fifteen minutes each, with follow-up appointments next week on any I need to see again. Oh, yeah, and there'll be a workman in to install another phone line. Stick with him in case he needs anything, okay?''

"Yes, sir.''

He sent her a sour look and raked his hand through his hair. "Look, I probably owe you an apology.''

"You do?''

"Do me another favor. Don't overdo the big-eyed in-genue act.'' Callie was wondering how he could have mis-led her aunt into believing he was so sweet and sensitive all these years when he went on to say, "How about dinner tomorrow night at Claire's? I'll pick you up about eight, will that give you time to get home and change?''

"Into what, a fairy princess? Sorry, I left my fairy dust back home in Yadkin County.''

Seven

The call came while Callie was watching the late news that night. Still clutching an apple core, she answered, expecting to hear Hank telling her he wouldn't be home until tomorrow.

"Callie, honey, is that you? This is Grace. Grace Spencer. I forgot all about the time difference. Is it later or earlier out there?"

"It's earlier, Grace. I just finished watching the news."

"Yes, well…it's the middle of the night here, and I hate like anything to have to tell you, but I didn't want you to hear it on the news or anything."

Oh, God, Mama and Daddy…

"I tried to get hold of your folks, but they're out of town."

Callie leaned back against the wall and closed her eyes in relief. "Grace, what's happened. Is it Doc? Did he—?"

"Not that I know of. Nobody's died or been hurt, so you can rest easy on that score, at least."

At least? A tornado. The Yadkin River had overflowed the banks, climbed the ridge and flooded her basement with mud.

"Grace, just tell me."

"Your house just burnt down. It's too dark to see much—the firemen are still there, but I don't think there's much left. Oh, honey, I'm just as sorry as I can be."

After a few more questions, Callie numbly replaced the phone. It could have been worse, she told herself. It could've been so much worse. Mama and Daddy, on the road in that old van of theirs...

Oh, Lord, what am I going to do now?

The first thing she did was make herself a cup of strong tea. It helped, if only in that waiting for the kettle to come to a boil gave her time to organize her thoughts.

I'll have to call...

Call who? Whom? What could anyone do?

She poured boiling water onto two tea bags and added three spoons of sugar. It was only a house. Nobody had been hurt...or worse. She tried to think, shook her head and grabbed the grocery pad and a pencil. She always thought better when she could see her thoughts take shape.

Number one: check on flights home. Number two: let Hank know so he could find someone to replace her.

Call Aunt Manie?

No, that could wait. There was no point in worrying her aunt now that her recovery was coming along so nicely. There wasn't a blessed thing she could do about it. It was Callie's house, Callie's responsibility. It was up to her to take care of it.

It's not just my house, it's my home! I just finished having it painted.

"My plants," she whimpered, instinctively filling her mind with small, unimportant details like fresh paint and sweet potato tops she'd rooted in water, that were crawling all over her kitchen windowsills. And the material she'd bought for when she had time to make new bathroom curtains. As long as she focused on small things, the larger ones couldn't creep up on her.

Hank had just opened his first file and poured his third cup of coffee when Callie trudged up the stairs the next morning. She was early. She looked like hell. Looked as if she hadn't slept in weeks.

"What's wrong, headache? Picked up a bug?"

"I have to go home. I thought about calling to tell you, but decided it's better to tell you in person. I, um—I have to go home."

"Sure, take off as long as you need. I can handle everything here."

"No, you don't understand, I have to go *home*. Back to North Carolina."

They were standing outside his doorway, in Manie's area. Hank took her arm, steered her inside and closed the door. "Want to tell me what's going on? Has something happened to one of your parents? I believe you mentioned that they travel a lot?"

"My parents? No, they're all right as far as I know. I haven't been able to get in touch with them, though, and I probably should."

"Give me the data, I'll—"

"My plane leaves at 11:10. It was the first one I could get that didn't have a long wait in Atlanta."

"Whoa, back up a step. Why can't you get in touch with your folks?"

"They're not home."

"Okay, they're not home. Do you have some idea where they might be? Is it important for you to reach them?"

"No. Yes. I guess so."

"Callie, what the devil's going on? You want to tell me about it?"

She shook her head. Her hair was short, but it was thick, curly and shiny, the color he'd heard referred to as dish-water-blond. It was anything but.

"I have a number written down where I can probably contact them later, but they haven't checked in yet and I have to leave in time to get to the airport, and—"

He redirected his line of questioning. "What airline?"

"I wrote it down. It's not one of the big lines."

"Cancel."

She gave him a look that managed to combine worry, exasperation and mystification, with an added dash of impatience. "Look, I don't have time for this. It's going to take me an hour to get to the airport, and they said I have to be there early. I just came by to let you know. I'll leave a list of your appointments for the rest of the week, but I have to—"

"Callie, sit down. Take a deep breath," he commanded, and such was the authority he projected, she did both. "Now, listen to me. I don't know what kind of emergency situation you're in, so unless we coordinate our efforts, we're both going to waste a lot of time and energy. First, I want you to give me whatever you know about how to locate your folks, and I'll put a man on it. Next, either you call and cancel your reservation or I will. Call Pete and tell him to prep for a flight to—what airport will we be flying into?"

Callie was shaking her head. "Stop it. I can't think when you come at me this way."

"Good. Let me do the thinking."

She suddenly blazed up at him, the flush in her cheeks overcoming the shadows around her eyes. "I said stop it! Stop trying to bulldoze me, I don't need it. I'm perfectly capable of doing whatever needs doing. If I depend on myself, I'll know what to expect."

"Meaning you don't trust me."

"Meaning—oh, I don't know what I mean, I only know that in an emergency I can count on me. Nobody else. I don't need anyone else, it only confuses me."

"Now, that I believe. Look at you, you're shaking."

"I am not! I'm—it's this darned air conditioner. It's cold as a walk-in freezer in here!" She yanked off her glasses, rubbed them angrily with the tail of her skirt and jammed them back on her face, but not before he caught a glimpse of the stricken look in her eyes.

"Ah, Callie..." He held out his arms, but she stiffened against the back of the chair.

"Don't. Don't touch me," she warned, taking another deep, shuddering breath. "All right then, if you know someone who knows how to locate people when they're on the road, you can give it a try, but that's all. And I'm only letting you do that much because—well, because I don't have time to go to the police or whoever and explain everything to them."

"Fair enough. Give me your numbers—make, color, model, license—whatever you have. I'll handle it. While I'm on the computer, I'll cancel your flight, and then we'll—"

"We, nothing. This is my problem, not yours. I'll handle it."

She was so brittle it hurt him to look at her. One wrong word and she was going to shatter into a million pieces. What the devil had happened to get her into this state?

More to the point, what had caused her to bottle up her

feelings so tightly that when they blew, she hadn't a clue as to how to handle them?

The phone rang, breaking the stillness. Hank snatched it up, listened for thirty seconds, and said, "No. Pansy, we just went over all this. Count me out."

The sound of a high-pitched voice could be heard going on and on. Never taking his gaze off Callie, he waited, holding the phone away from his ear, and then he said into a momentary lull, "I'll call you in a day or so. We'll sort it out then."

He hung up the phone, then lifted it off the receiver and laid it on the desk. As if waiting for the air to clear, neither of them moved, neither of them spoke. Warily they eyed each other, senses heightened to flashpoint.

Hank studied the woman before him, trying vainly to hang onto his objectivity. She was so damn young, with all the pride and vulnerability of the young. He tried to remember what he'd felt like at that age. Had he ever been that young? As the richest kid in town, he'd been pretty well hamstrung when it came to proving his mettle. Whatever his achievements growing up, he could never be sure his old man's wealth and influence hadn't tainted the outcome.

At least Callie didn't have that particular handicap to overcome. By the time he'd been the age she was now, he'd already already gone through a marriage, an annulment, a stint in the service and a couple of wars. The press referred to them as police actions, but when someone was shooting live ammo at him, he damned well called it war.

According to Manie, Callie had worked in the office of a G.P. in some bucolic little paradise where everyone was on a first-name basis. Mayberry, U.S.A. So what the hell had happened there last night to cause her to come unglued this morning?

He was tempted to pry it out of her, but instead he said, "Give me whatever you have, Callie, and I'll get someone onto tracking down your parents."

She fumbled in her purse and came up with an address book. "If you get in touch, tell them to meet me..." He waited, hurting for her. She shook her head again and whispered hopelessly, "I have to go home."

"I know, honey. I'm going to get you there as quickly as possible."

"I hate flying."

"It'll take three days to drive."

"Four," she corrected politely, but he could tell by the glittery look in her eyes that her heart wasn't up to arguing the point.

"Once we take off, you won't even know you're flying. You can sleep the whole way and wake up on the ground. That way you'll be nice and rested when we tackle whatever it is together."

If she'd let him help her. He'd never met a women who kept a tighter rein on herself.

He saw a chink in her armor and dived in. "What about Manie?"

"Do you think I should tell her? It's not like there's anything she could do."

"Callie, I don't even know what this is all about, remember? All I know is you've suddenly got to be somewhere else, and I'm doing my damnedest to get you there. I can't help you make your decisions unless you turn over a little more information."

She dug a notepad out of the pocket of her tan, wraparound skirt and frowned at it. He watched her weigh the pros and cons and tried to read her mind. Had he thought of her as drab? Colorless? She was neither. Subtle, yes.

Picturing Pansy, monochromatic from the tips of her

beige Brunos to the top of her sleek, blond pageboy, he thought about the differences between the two women. For some obscure reason, Callie tried to play down her feminine attractions, but there was nothing she could do about that elfin quality that was so at odds with an almost military sense of organized efficiency. The combination was lethal. Even now it was beginning to fire up all sorts of inappropriate responses, both physical and mental.

"My house burned down last night."

"Come again?" It took a moment for the words to sink in.

"I said my house burned down. To the ground. The only thing left standing is the chimneys. There are—there were—th-three of them."

"Ah, hell—ah, Callie—oh, baby..."

Somehow, Callie found herself in his arms. Somehow, her glasses left her face, and she was swallowing hard, trying to choke back the tears. Her throat ached with the effort, but she refused to cry all over his custom-tailored, open-neck, Western-cut denim shirt.

His hand continued to stroke her shoulders, to ruffle her hair, and all the while his voice was a deep, soothing rumble, like a bear growling deep inside a cave. "Ah, honey... Shh, it's going to be all right, we'll fix it. Whatever it takes, we'll make it right. Shh, don't cry so hard, you'll get a headache."

"I'm not crying," she declared, the words muffled against his chest. As if to prove it, she leaned back in his arms and glared at him, fighting against the need to allow someone else to shoulder her burdens for once in her life.

It wouldn't do. She didn't dare, not with this man. "I never cry," she said, and swallowed past the painful lump in her throat.

There, she told herself, slipping from his arms. She felt

better now. The last thing she needed was another distraction. First Manie's surgery, then her house burning, and now...

And anyway, he was only being kind. He was that kind of man. She'd watched him the night of the ball, taking time to speak to every woman on dowager row, taking the time to reassure that poor terrified waiter, dancing with the woman in the pink dress. She was just another employee. What was it the pink lady had called her? A charity case?

If only it were that simple.

"Yes, well...I'd better try one last time to get in touch with Mama and Daddy. There's this place in Nashville where they usually hang out called Catgut's."

The rain started about halfway to the private airport outside Royal. Hank muttered something about a freaky aftermath of the big El Niño and the La Niña that followed.

Callie said, "Oh, no, we'll have to wait."

"It's only rain. The Avenger's waterproof."

It wasn't only rain, it was thunder, the low, growly type that sounded like a freight train circling the town, but there was no visible lightning. Hank did his best to reassure her, but she was already beginning to get that queasy feeling.

"It's going to be all right, honey. Planes are designed to fly in all kinds of weather. Would I risk damaging the Avenger?" He chuckled, but she knew it was only to reassure her. "Take a deep breath."

"I'm already hyperventilating. It makes me dizzy."

"Okay, then count from two hundred and eleven, backward."

"Do you realize that my whole life is spinning out of control? Counting isn't going to help that!"

"Nice going. You're yelling at me. Now try cursing.

You know any good words? I can help you out if you need a few."

"Heck, darn, spit."

"Is that how you do it in Carolina? Here in Texas, we say—"

"I know what you say. I know what you're trying to do, too, don't think I don't."

"Is it working?"

She bit her lip, blinked and nodded. "I guess it must be."

"Trust me," he said, and she discovered, somewhat to her amazement, that she did.

Hank made two quick calls on the way to the airport. Distracted, Callie didn't even try to follow the conversation. By half past ten they were in the air. A few minutes later, they were above the clouds, and she would have wept with relief, only they were still flying, and anyone with a grain of common sense knew that things heavier than air fell to the ground. Even birds were designed with hollow bones to cut down on the weight. They probably took a deep breath and held it every time they launched themselves from a tree limb.

This thing—this Avenger—didn't have a hollow bone in its body. Sleek as a bullet, it was so luxurious she was almost afraid to relax for fear of spilling the drink Hank had placed in her hand before they took off. She'd sniffed it, detected alcohol and decided she'd be better off abstaining. If they were going to crash hundreds of miles from civilization in the middle of the Texas desert, she would need all her wits about her.

Hank had assured her it was safe. He was a pilot, he'd told her, even if he wasn't flying the plane himself today. That meant they had two pilots. Two pilots, one plane, one passenger. That improved the odds, didn't it?

Lordy, this thing was unbelievable! She'd flown coach once, to Norfolk, to her mother's brother's wedding. It was nothing at all like this.

There was an office, a kitchen, a bedroom and two bathrooms. This, she supposed, was the living room. There was a sofa. There were tables inlaid in a checkerboard pattern, and deep, cushiony chairs. There was even a vase of fresh flowers on a desk under the windows.

Hank had settled her in, fastened a tapestry seat belt across her lap, handed her a drink and a copy of the *Midland Reporter-Telegram*, and disappeared behind a teak-paneled door in the front of the plane.

Didn't they have a flight attendant? She could have done with some female companionship. Someone who wouldn't consider her weak for falling apart.

The plane lurched. Her drink sloshed. Callie squealed and gripped the armrests.

"How's it going?" asked Hank, emerging from the front room, or whatever they called the little room up front where the driver sat.

He sat down beside her, slinging one leg over the other. Manie said damp weather always made his leg hurt, that he'd been injured in a crash in the Persian Gulf. Callie wondered if he was hurting now, considering a light mist of rain had been falling when they'd left Royal. She probably ought to offer him sympathy, but she didn't have that much to spare.

"You haven't touched your drink," he noticed.

"I didn't need it."

His smile was teasing, making her feel about five years old.

"How long before we get there?"

The plane chose that moment to drop like a rock, sending

Callie's heart into her throat. She shut her eyes and whimpered.

"Clear air turbulence. We'll be out of it in no time."

She squeaked out a question, her eyes still tightly closed. "Are we going to crash?"

"You know, it's a fascinating thing, clear air turbulence. They're getting a real good handle on it. At this altitude there's no real danger, but if it'll make you feel any safer, the Avenger is equipped with state-of-the-art technology. She's got a fifteen-second warning of any air turbulence ahead."

"Fifteen *seconds?*" Her eyes were still closed.

"At the speed we're moving, that's more than enough time to take evasive action."

"Then why didn't we evade it?"

He didn't bother to tell her that the technology was still brand-new. That there were still a few bugs. That sometimes a sudden, evasive action could be just as turbulent.

They experienced another small quiver, and then the flight smoothed out, as if they were floating in a swimming pool. "Open your eyes, honey."

In a tight little gesture, she shook her head. "Tell me when it's over. I'll look then."

Over the muted drone of two powerful jet engines, she heard the faint sound of his breathing, felt the warmth of his body caress her sweat-damp skin. Something soft and moist and warm brushed her mouth, and every instinct in her body urged her to lean forward. If it hadn't been for the seat belt holding her in place, she'd have wrapped herself around him tighter than kudzu on a dead pine tree.

Light filled the cabin. Heat filled her body. Something that felt like electricity filled her senses as he twisted his head to deepen the area of contact, only it was far warmer, mellower, than any mere electrical current could possibly be.

If there was another world outside the haven of Hank's arms, it ceased to exist. She was vaguely aware of the feel of his hands on her lap, and then there was a click and he lifted her right up out of her chair and swung her onto the sofa.

A shaft of sunlight slanted across the cabin like a benediction. Callie murmured something irrelevant, and then he was kissing her again, and this time she was fully aware of where she was, who she was with, and what they were doing.

And none of it mattered. She was miles off the ground, in the arms of a man whose sex appeal and womanizing were legendary, and none of it seemed to matter.

She felt his tongue on her throat, and then she felt his touch on her breast. "Oh, wait—no—I don't think—" She gasped for air and tried again. "That is, I'm all right now, so you don't have to—I mean, we shouldn't—"

"Shh. It's all right, Callie. We'll talk about it later, whenever you're ready. Looks like smooth flying weather now, all the way to PTI."

"Piedmont Triangle? But that's in Greensboro."

"So?"

"But I live in Yadkin County."

"So we'll rent a car and drive. It's practically next door."

"By Texas rules, you mean."

He grinned, and Callie had a feeling she was in far more trouble than she'd suspected. Her parents she could deal with. Insurance agents, too, if she had to.

Hank Langley, with that wicked gleam in his eyes, was something else again.

Eight

Leaving Pete to secure the plane, Hank rented a car, picked up a map and asked Callie where she wanted to stop for lunch.

"I'm not hungry."

"Sure you are."

"Stop trying to manage me."

"Someone has to. You're not doing such a great job on your own," he said laconically.

She came to a complete halt in the middle of the concourse, oblivious to the crowds hurrying past on all sides. Just once—just *once*—she'd like to rattle his cage, she really would. "I'm managing just fine, thank you. Now come on, we still have a long drive ahead."

"Have you thought about where we're going to put up for the night? Is there a decent hotel in this little town of yours?"

She opened her mouth and closed it. Home. She'd been going home. But her home was no longer there.

It was as if the sun had just slipped behind a cloud.

"Callie, stop fighting me. You're as brittle as thin ice. Ease up and let me get you through the next few hours. Then, once you've got your land legs under you, you can take over and run the entire show single-handedly. Do we have a deal?"

People were looking at them.

Correction: they were looking at Henry Harrison Langley, III. He was well worth looking at, with his lean, angular face, his lean, rugged body encased in lean, boot-top jeans and a Western-cut shirt. How could any man who'd been born into money look so tough, so self-sufficient? Weren't the idle rich supposed to be soft and spoiled?

Hank wasn't soft. If he was spoiled, it was only from having women chasing after him constantly. He didn't play golf. He didn't play tennis. Even when he appeared to be idle, that steel-trap brain of his was clicking away at the speed of sound.

"Callie? Do we have a deal? Ah, hell, you're still feeling queasy, aren't you?"

"I never felt queasy."

"Uh-huh."

Taking her arm, he steered her toward the exit. The glass-and-steel double doors slid noiselessly open, as if eager to do his bidding.

"I guess I wouldn't mind ginger ale and some crackers," she allowed. "Not because I'm queasy, just to tide me over." He gave her that all-seeing look that made her feel as if he could read the labels in the back of her shirt.

So she was queasy. So maybe she should've eaten something before they took off. Heaven knows, she wouldn't have dared once they were in the air. She hadn't even thought to stop and eat breakfast before they left, she'd been so busy making lists of what needed doing before she closed up Aunt Manie's house: who needed to be contacted, what she needed to pack to go home, what could be left behind.

If there was one thing Callie prided herself on being, it was organized. Organized and efficient. And responsible. Which was three things, actually.

Mama left the windows open, but I'd better close all but those on the porch, because it's going to rain.

Mama said make a bologna sandwich, but it's got that shiny green look. Peanut butter and banana would be safer.

Daddy said he was out of shaving cream, I'd better add it to the shopping list. Oh, shoot, he forgot to leave me any money today for the class trip.

Oh, yes, Callie had several admirable qualities, only somewhere between Texas and Carolina, the portion of her brain that drove her common sense seemed to have blown a circuit.

"You need more than a snack, what you need is a good solid meal."

"Quit trying to force-feed me, if I need more than crackers I'll tell you, all right?" He'd offered her lunch aboard the plane, but her stomach had been turning somersaults before they'd ever left the ground. And that was before all the air turbulence. Before he'd kissed her. On a turbulence scale of one-to-ten, the kiss alone was an easy fifteen.

They were on I-40 headed west when her stomach started to rumble. Hank didn't say a word, he just pulled off at the next exit and cruised slowly along a strip lined with fast-food outlets. "What'll it be, burgers, dogs, subs? If you'd rather, we can find something more substantial."

"Oh, all right, if you're that hungry I guess I might as well have a little something, too." She wouldn't be able to choke down more than a few bites, but at least it would keep him from nagging her.

Her stomach growled again. She shot him a sidelong look. He was grinning, darn him. Neither of them said a word as he turned into a familiar franchise, followed the line of traffic to the drive-up window and placed an order for two bacon-cheeseburgers, two orders of fries, a milk and a large iced tea.

He paid. She didn't argue. She didn't even want to think what the trip across country in a private jet had cost. Did people still get thrown into debtor's prison, or did they simply declare bankruptcy? She couldn't even afford to ask.

Hank pulled the rental car under a big shady oak tree on the edge of the parking lot. Leaving the engine running and the air conditioner fighting the ninety-eight-degree temperature, he opened the sack and parceled out the food.

"I can't eat all this."

"Eat what you want and feed the rest to the sparrows." Eyes masked behind wraparound sunglasses, he leaned back against the door and studied the small woman in the wilted cotton outfit. She was too pale. Even her lips were pale.

Her lips…

She took the first tentative nibble as if she expected the cheeseburger to bite back. The second nibble was larger, the third was downright enthusiastic. A few minutes later she crumpled the wrapper, sighed, popped the last French fry into her mouth and daintily wiped her fingers on the paper napkin.

"Thank you."

"You're welcome."

Cool and collected again, she refastened her seat belt, folded her hands in her lap and waited for him to get it in gear. Feeling an unholy urge to shake her loose from that false composure she wore like a coronation robe, he told himself he'd give a block of stock to find out what was going on inside her head.

Thank God she didn't know what was going on inside his. What was going on inside his jeans was bad enough. It was downright embarrassing. He was nearly forty years old, long past the age of instant, irrational lust. Callie was twenty-two. If he was any judge of women—and among his close friends, he was considered something of an expert—her sexual experience was negligible, if not nil. He'd heard of middle-aged men losing their minds, chasing after kids half their age. He'd always thought they were pretty damned pathetic.

Callie stirred restlessly. "If you're ready to leave, we'd better get going. This time of day, traffic on I-40 between here and Winston is pretty hectic. Once we turn off onto 421, it'll be some better, but not a whole lot."

"You're the boss."

"I'd like that in writing, please. Notarized."

"What, my word's not good enough?"

"Actually it is. I guess I'm just not used to having people take over my responsibilities." She sounded surprised, maybe even a little pleased.

"Relax and enjoy it."

"Ha."

But she did. At least she was no longer gripping her fingers in a white-knuckled knot. He had a feeling she hadn't slept since the call had come in. Those shadows under her eyes were a sure tip-off. The look of fragility that made him want to feed her, shelter her, protect her, even though he knew damned well that sleep or no sleep, she was a lot tougher than she looked.

So why did he keep thinking of her as tender?

Why did the word describe the way he felt about her? One of several ways.

Hank pulled off the highway at a truck stop and studied the sleeping woman beside him. He'd removed her glasses once she'd dozed off. Without them, she looked as vulnerable as a fledgling bird. He hated to wake her, but unless the map was wrong, they were about to run out of county. He needed instructions on how to locate this house of hers.

Or at least locate the place where it had stood for more than a century, according to Manie, before it burned to the ground.

Hank had called her from the plane. He hadn't told Callie about it yet. He'd intended to, but then Greg had called to say that Blake would be getting in by the end of the week, and Sterling was already reorganizing the details. As CEO of Churchill Enterprises, Sterling was used to running the show, but then so was Hank. In some cases, too many Alpha males could be a problem, but this mission was going to call for men who could think on their feet and weren't afraid to improvise at a moment's notice.

So he hadn't told Callie about Manie, and then they'd hit that rough patch and he'd had to ease her fears and somehow, things had gotten out of hand.

Callie began to stir. "Wha...are we there yet?"

"I thought you might need a pit stop. I got a couple of cold drinks out of the machine. We're in Yadkin County, but I'm not sure just where. Want to give me some directions?"

"I'd better freshen up first."

"Take your time."

On the way back she stopped inside and bought a couple of candy bars. Handing him one, she peeled the paper off the other and took a dainty nibble off one corner. Hell, even her teeth turned him on.

"Get back on the highway, take the next exit we come to, head north, go about a mile and a half and take the first left. About a quarter of a mile farther you'll come to Riley Road. That's Grandpop's."

The acrid smell of smoke seeped through the car's ventilation system long before they turned off onto Riley Road. Passing a gray modular home with a plastic swing set and a pickup truck in the front yard, they continued to the end of the graveled road, straddling ruts and dodging potholes caused by recent rains and heavy traffic.

It was devastating. Trees that had stood even longer than the house had been badly scorched, a few burned black. What might once have been a fine old lawn had been completely churned up by a variety of heavy firefighting equipment. Drink cans and food wrappers had been carelessly tossed out, possibly by neighbors who'd come to see what they could do to help. More likely by gawkers, drawn like ambulance chasers to any spectacle.

He heard her sharply indrawn breath. She was gripping his thigh, leaning across him for a better view, and he was tempted to make a fast three-point turn and get her the hell away. But he couldn't do that. Not even if she'd allow it. Aside from the practical angle, she needed closure.

"The chimneys," she whispered. "Grace said they were still standing last night. Was it only last night?"

"They're still here, standing guard." Standing guard over what? God, he sounded like a two-bit philosopher. Clearing his throat, he made a stab at something a little more down to earth. "Good masonry," he said, as if that could somehow make up for the loss of everything else.

There were three of them, one of rock, two of brick, standing tall and desolate amidst the blackened, still smoking rubble. Callie said, "I have to get out."

Wordlessly he nodded, and got out to stand beside her. For what seemed hours they gazed out over the scene of desecration. Charred timbers. Shattered glass. Twisted metal—some short lengths of pipe, a section of gutter. A few blackened appliances.

It was still light, but the sun had already disappeared behind a low ridge of haze-shrouded mountains in the distance. The air, hot and thick with humidity, was that peculiar shade of dusky gold. He wanted her away from here. Maybe he should've let her fly commercial. At least that way, by the time she got here the ruins might've stopped smoking.

But he couldn't let her come alone. She needed him, and as crazy as it was, he needed to be here with her. "Callie, there's nothing we can do here until things cool off."

"It was lavender."

"What was lavender?"

"My house. I tried to think of it as gray because lavender sounds sort of odd for a house, but that's what it was. It was called Hawaiian Heliotrope. I got a real good deal on the paint because nobody else wanted it. Sixty percent off. That's the only reason I could afford it without going into debt, which I hate like anything to do. I don't even own a credit card. Oh, and I painted the kitchen wing myself, did I tell you? It was only one story, so I could reach it with a stepladder. I was going to have the wiring redone next, but—" A stricken look came over her. He started to tell her it wasn't her fault, but she didn't give him time. "But Grace said they had an awful storm, with lots of lightning and all. She said she heard a transformer blow up, so maybe..."

She swallowed audibly. He wished she'd just break down and cry and get it over with, because nonstop talking wasn't going to get the job done. Sooner or later, she was going to have to come up for air, and when she did it would still be there waiting for her. The ashes of all her dreams.

He interrupted her flow of words. "What do you say we check into a hotel, maybe have room service bring up something light, and then first thing in the morning we can get down to business?"

"Did I tell you what color I painted the trim? It was called Barn Red, but it was a sort of dark maroon, a little bit on the rusty side. It looked great with Hawaiian Heliotrope. The paint people said it was an inspired choice. I was thinking about maybe saving up for storm windows once I get another job, but..."

Ah, jeez, he didn't know how to handle this. Didn't she have anyone to step in and take over? Where the devil was her father? Where was her mother? Manie had said when he'd talked to her earlier that Bain and Sally Riley wouldn't be much help, that they'd married too young, buckled under the responsibility of having a child, and finally gone to seed. He still didn't know what she'd meant by that last, but dammit, Callie needed family at a time like this. She needed a mother to urge her to cry and a father to tell her it was all right and make her believe it. There was nothing *he* could do. He had no business even getting involved.

Too late. He was already involved. And he had no one to blame but himself. "Come on, time to go. You can tell me all about it on the way back to town."

The fact that she didn't argue only made him more uneasy. He'd seen similar reactions over the years, sometimes immediate, but often delayed for weeks after the trauma occurred.

"Honey, it's rough, I know, but you're doing fine. Manie would be proud of you."

That prompted a high squeaky whimper.

"Hey, I know for a fact that you Riley women are fa-

mous for keeping your cool under trying circumstances."
Sure they were, and the Langley men were famous for
spreading it on with a front-end loader. "I guess that
sounded pretty patronizing, huh? I didn't mean it that way.
Look, I'm just a little out of my depth here, so help me
out, will you? Tell me where to go."

He hadn't intended to give her the opening, but it
worked. At least that shell-shocked look began to fade. She
blinked up at him. "You're asking me to tell you where to
go?"

"Where to get off? Uh, maybe I'd better rephrase that."

"No, don't. Let me think a minute."

He wanted to see her smile. He wanted to hear her laugh,
even at his expense. He wanted her, period, and he was
used to getting what he wanted. Patience was not one of
his major attributes.

Fortunately—or unfortunately—scruples were.

"All right, go to the end of this road and take a left.
Then go about a mile and a half and take a right on an
unpaved road. It's a shortcut. It'll get us back on the highway."

"That's it? You're not going to take a free shot at me?"

"We're in North Carolina now," she said sweetly.
"Texas rules don't apply here."

He took a three-room suite, giving her a sense of privacy,
but assuring that he'd be within easy reach if she needed
him. Hank told himself that was the only reason he hadn't
booked separate rooms, on separate floors, at opposite ends
of the hotel. He almost managed to convince himself.

It was a mark of Callie's distraction that she didn't even
question his choice. "You'd probably like to shower and
change. How about dinner? Downstairs, on the town, or
room service?"

"I think I'll just go to bed."

"Think again. You'll sleep a lot better after a hot bath and a good meal. I'll help with either...or both. Your choice."

"Then order me something to eat while I get a shower. I need to try and reach Mama again before I go to bed, and I guess I'd better talk to Aunt Manie."

He gave that one a pass. "Steak? Chicken? Oatmeal?"

She made a face at him. He figured it was a good sign.

She was the only woman he'd ever known who could eat chicken with her fingers and still manage to look dainty. He told her so just to see if he could lure another smile out of hiding.

"Aunt Manie eats with her fingers."

"Steak, maybe, but never chicken." Hell, he'd do knock-knock jokes if it would make her smile.

"Hank, I'm too tired to sit around talking. I guess I can wait to talk to Aunt Manie, but I really do need to try Mama and Daddy again before I go to bed. I warned you, they're not easy to find when they're on the road."

She had that right. He'd had his people calling all over three states without turning up anything. At least they weren't on record as being in jail or in any of the major hospitals.

"I've left a call for six in the morning. This is—oh, for heaven's sake, I don't even know what day of the week it is."

He told her, and she said, "Then that gives me plenty of time to meet with the insurance people. I'd better rent myself a car, first thing, so that—"

"Whoa. Back up a minute, will you? Is there something wrong with my rental? You want something flashier?"

She sent him the kind of look that crack deserved.

"You'll need yours to get back to the airport, unless you'd rather take the shuttle. I'm pretty sure the hotel has one, but I'd still rather rent something on my own, that way the paperwork doesn't get all messed up when I turn it in."

A muscle in his jaw twitched, that was all. It wasn't the first time he'd picked his way through a minefield. "I'll split the last of the wine with you, then I'm going to grab a shower while you try your numbers one more time. After that we'll settle whatever needs settling before we turn in."

She took a sip of the wine and wrinkled her nose. "I can't decide about Aunt Manie. I hate to have to explain over the phone, but if she tries to reach me at her house, she might worry."

"I called her from the plane."

"You didn't tell me that." She looked more hurt than angry, so he reached out and cupped her chin. Tender. Yeah, that was a good word.

"You weren't feeling particularly conversational, if you'll remember. Besides, there's nothing much to tell. She's doing fine, playing cards and watching baseball, taking it easy. She says don't worry about her plants, they can take care of themselves for a few days."

He didn't bother to add that she'd given him her unflattering opinion of Callie's parents, tried to pry loose a few answers as to the status of what she called the Hank Stakes and made him promise to look after Callie, who according to Manie wasn't nearly as self-sufficient as she thought she was. He could always tell when Manie was up to something. A thousand miles or so did little to allay the feeling.

He left Callie seated at the desk, a glass of merlot in one hand, telephone in the other, the telephone book open before her. Wearing the hotel's thick white terry-cloth bathrobe, with a towel around her head, she looked about fourteen.

Hands off, Langley. What you need is waiting for you back in Texas.

Yeah, but what he wanted was sitting right here in a hotel in North Carolina, halfway between a pair of king-size beds.

Hank cracked open the bathroom door to allow the steam to escape while he buttoned on a clean shirt. Callie was still talking on the phone. "—but Mama—no, I didn't think to ask. No, I haven't called him yet, but I'm fixing to right now. I'll probably be seeing him sometime tomorrow if he can fit me in. Tell Daddy that I said— What? That's real nice, but, Mama—"

Hank emerged from his room in time to see her carefully replace the phone. He didn't like the look on her face. "I see you finally managed to reach your folks," he said carefully. His hair was still wet. He'd cut himself shaving, something he hadn't done in years.

"That was Mama."

"So I gathered. Will they be joining us here?"

"At the hotel, you mean? No, they have a loft in one of the old factory buildings. Anyway, they can't make it. Daddy won a best-in-show with a slab-built teapot and he's being interviewed tomorrow by some big crafts magazine, and the group's booked studio time to make a demo."

"Wow. That's great…I guess. What about the house?"

She looked away, that lost expression creeping back again. "I can handle everything. It's my responsibility. Mama said if I'll take care of the details, they'll split the insurance with me."

He waited two beats to see if she was going to throw something. "Callie, that doesn't even make sense."

She shrugged. "They've got their minds on other things.

It's really important, making a demo and being interviewed and all.''

''Correct me if I'm wrong, but didn't that house belong to you, not your parents? In that case, whatever the settlement is, it's yours. Aside from all that, they damn well ought to be here for you.''

''I don't need them.'' The tip of her nose turned red, and then her eyes began to fill. ''I don't need you, either. I don't need anybody, I keep telling you that!''

Nine

When the dam broke, Hank was there for her. He told himself while she drenched his clean shirt, the only spare he'd brought with him, that in lieu of her parents, his arms were better than no arms at all.

He held her close, breathing in the light, lemony fragrance of her hair, the soapy scent of her skin as their two bodies, clinging tightly, began to generate heat of a different kind.

This is Callie, man. Lay a finger on her and Manie's going to kill you.

Too late. He'd already laid both hands on her. He only hoped she was too inexperienced to realize what was happening to him. Although if she'd ever studied basic biology, there was no way she could miss it. He was fully, embarrassingly, almost painfully aroused.

He tried his best to keep his hands on her back, stroking waist to shoulders and back again, with a few pats along the way. The towel had fallen from her damp hair, and he combed his fingers through the short, tangled strands.

Wet silk. Wet, warm and curly. Before he could shut it off, his mind began screening pictures of a naked Callie, lying sprawled across the sheets, wet, warm and waiting.

Her small breasts were crushed against his chest. Even through the thick terry-cloth robe he could feel her nipples, or imagine he did, which was just as bad. Worse. Imagination was the headiest of all aphrodisiacs.

Callie was a noisy cryer. She might be neat, quiet and efficient in all other respects, but when it came to crying, she cut loose with both barrels.

"I'm ss-s-orry," she blubbered. "I'm so sorry, this is so embarrassing."

"Hush. Shh, let it out. Cuss a little if it'll help. I'll even help you."

She sniffed and drew back, gave him a suspicious look and then hid her face on his chest again.

He did a Manie-like *tsk-tsk* sound with his teeth and tongue and said, "Don't you just hate bawling? It's so messy."

Her shoulders quivered. She either sniffed or snickered, he wasn't sure which, and asked him if he had a tissue.

He dug out his handkerchief. Luckily it was a clean one. "Will this do?"

She used it efficiently and effectively, took a deep breath and said, "Now I owe you a shirt and a clean handkerchief. I'm really sorry, Hank, I don't usually do this sort of thing."

"No problem. Glad to be of service."

"Yes, well…speaking of service, I don't know how I'll ever be able to pay you for the trip and the room and everything. Maybe when the insurance claim is settled—"

His fingers bit into her shoulders. "Stop it. Dammit, Callie, don't say things like that, not to me. We're friends, aren't we?"

"Are we?"

The question hung there between them, stark and revealing. With another woman, he might have thought she was playing games, but not Callie. Games weren't her style.

There were several answers he might have given her, all of which would be truthful up to a point, but not the whole truth. The whole truth was, she aroused him as no woman ever had, and not just sexually.

And that was the scary part. He didn't want to think about it, but such was the power of her direct gaze that he found himself trying to explain. "Callie, I'd have been your friend for Manie's sake, no matter what. She happens to be the closest thing to family I've got left. You're important to me because you're important to her."

Which was true, as far as it went. It was what lay beyond that point that was tying him in knots. "Look, you're not the only one who has claims on her," he said impatiently. "Deal with it."

Her face was far too expressive. Reading the doubts piling up behind those clear, silver-blue eyes, he forced a lighter note. "All I'm trying to say is that even if you'd turned out to be a real jerk, I'd have been your friend for Manie's sake. Lucky for me, you turned out to be…the way you turned out to be. Which is pretty fine."

"You don't have to explain, I know you've had her a lot longer than I have, and you don't have to pay me extravagant compliments."

Extravagant compliments. Right. He thought of Pansy's voracious appetite for compliments, the way Bianca's ego constantly demanded its due. "You think I'm coming on too strong? How about if I say you turned out okay?"

"You don't have to tease me out of the sulks, either. I'm not a child."

"Honey, that's part of the trouble."

"I don't understand."

"Yeah, I think you do, but I'm getting the cart before the horse. For a Texan, that's damn near a felony."

Quiver of a smile. Flash of silver in those big, troubled eyes. So far, so good. He settled onto a rose-brocaded love seat, trying to look as if he weren't picturing her naked in his bed. "Like I said, you're the kind of woman I'd seriously like to have as a friend. You with me, so far?" She nodded. "So when a friend's in trouble, a true friend does what he can to help, right?" Another nod. "And you're in trouble."

"Oh, but I—"

"Nothing you can't handle," he hastened to say in deference to her pride. "But as long as I'm in a position to help out—" Dammit, he hadn't set out on this mission with seduction in mind. The trouble was, he couldn't be around her long and not think about it. "As long as we're here alone together—"

"That's an oxymoron."

"A what?"

"You can't be together and alone at the same time."

"Dammit, Callie, you know what I'm trying to say." Patience and arousal were a tough combination. Talk about your oxymorons. "You're a woman. A very attractive woman, even with your eyes red from crying and a bathrobe big enough to swallow you. I—I'm attracted to you, dammit!" *Great going, Langley. Climb out of one buffalo wallow and stumble into an even deeper one.*

"Well, you don't have to swear at me. I'm attracted to you, too, but then, I guess that's not too surprising. You're a—a nice-looking man."

Slowly he shook his head. Why her? Why had he managed to get himself involved with the one woman in all the world genetically engineered to drive him up a tree?

Rising abruptly, he began to pace. A vein throbbed at his temple. His leg was aching. Boots that had been custom-made for his feet began to chafe, and he knew damned well his zipper wasn't rated for this much pressure.

And there she sat, like a—like he didn't know what, telling him in that soft, husky drawl of hers that she was attracted to him, too. Not to his money. Not even to his social position, which in Royal, Texas, wasn't all that outstanding. Him. Hank Langley, the man.

"So?" Cautiously he asked, "What do you think we should do about it?"

"I haven't thought it through yet. What do you think we should do about it?"

"Nothing!" he fairly shouted. "Not one damned thing. Maybe if we ignore it, it'll die a natural death."

"What if it doesn't?"

"Honey, I'm old enough to be your father, don't you understand?"

She nodded. "In a way, I almost wish you were, but mostly, I'm glad you're not."

Baffled, he could only stare at her. "What's that supposed to mean?" She gnawed on her bottom lip, and once again he found his imagination shifting into overdrive.

"Just that you'd make a wonderful father, but if you were mine, then we wouldn't be having this conversation, would we?"

"You want to run that one by me again?"

Sighing, she tugged up the collar of her robe where it had slipped, baring one delicate, satin-skinned shoulder. "I'm not stupid, Hank. I know you'd like to sleep with me. I know that bothers you, because of Manie and because…well, just because. But I also know that's not the reason you're being so helpful. Driving me to Midland the other day. Flying me here. Being so nice and all." He bit off a mild oath, which she ignored. "The thing is, I'd like it, too, a whole lot, only I've never done this kind of thing before, and I'd probably make a mess of it, and right now I don't need another mess in my life. Do you understand?"

Closing his eyes, he took a deep breath and counted to ten. It didn't help. When he opened them again she was still there, still looking at him as if he were the answer to all her prayers, and he wasn't. Not the kind of prayers any decent young woman with high standards and untarnished ideals should be praying.

"Honey, don't tempt me too far. I'm no saint."

"You're not?"

There, she was doing it to him again. That quicksilver twinkle in her eyes. That hint, almost too subtle to catch, of laughter running just underneath her soft voice. He'd been sucker-punched before, but not since he was in grade school. And never by someone smaller and softer than he was.

"Damn you," he growled, "I'll teach you to play games with your elders!" Two strides and he was leaning over her, hauling her up into his arms. She didn't even try to resist him. Her hair was almost dry now, and it tickled his chin as she buried her face in his throat.

Hank told himself he was only teaching her a much-needed lesson about playing with fire, but he knew better. He could've sent her here with Pete. He hadn't had to come with her. It wasn't as if she were a stranger in a strange town, she had friends here. She'd have handled it on her own.

She settled into his arms as if she'd been made to fit him. Her face felt cool to touch, her breath against his skin warm and sweet. She gave a shuddering little sigh and snuggled against him as if she'd finally come home, and that did it. The last gleam of reason flickered and died.

Swinging her up into his arms, he made for the bedroom. Somewhere—in his shaving kit, probably—he had protection. Not because he'd expected to need it, but because he never traveled without it. With every intention of doing the responsible thing, he lowered her gently onto the bed. "I'll be right back," he whispered.

"Don't leave me. Oh, please—" Catching him by the shoulders, she drew him down over her. The position was uncomfortable. Bracing one knee on the bed beside her, he leaned over to kiss her once before he took care of business.

She opened to him like a hungry bird. Her fingers moved eagerly, awkwardly over his chest, tugging at buttons, lighting brush fires that rapidly spread out of control. Dragging himself away, he shrugged off his shirt and tossed it aside, his only thought to feel her naked body against his. By the time he lowered himself onto the bed again, he was shaking badly, struggling to regain control.

"You're not helping," he told her, but as his mouth was moving over her throat, she might not have heard him. Her hands fluttered down as far as his waist, exploring, stroking, tugging at the thick ribbon of dark hair that arrowed down into his jeans, then up again to the tufts that surrounded his nipples. Her fingers brushed over him there, sending an electrical charge jolting through his body, bringing him perilously close to the edge.

Somewhere in the deepest recesses of his mind, someone was chanting a warning. He ignored it. It was all he could do to keep on breathing. Her hand moved to his buckle, hesitated and then moved down to cover him. The part of him that was already swollen painfully hard, swelled even more to fill her hot palm.

Of their own volition his hips began to move against her hand. He groaned, drowning in the urgent need to drive himself inside her, the blind need to find release.

Slow down, slow down, slow down...

He covered her hand with his and dragged it up to his lips to suckle her fingertips. "Darling, we'd better slow down, or it will be all over." His voice was rough, harsh, that of a stranger. "Let me see you." With trembling hands he spread the lapels of her voluminous robe. Her skin was like cream, pale, rich, incredibly soft. He already knew her breasts were small, but he could never have imagined their perfection. Her deep rose nipples stood shyly, proudly erect. He kissed each one in turn, heard her gasp and stroked her with his tongue while his free hand tugged at the tie of her robe and spread it apart. The heady scent of arousal drifted around them like incense, spicy, musky, wildly intoxicating.

He held her eyes with his, needing to see every nuance of expression as he moved his hand slowly down from her breast, seeking the shadowy triangle nestled between her thighs.

His palms felt leathery against her tender flesh. When he encountered dry white cotton instead of warm, moist curls, his throat tightened with an emotion that hovered somewhere between tears and laughter. He didn't even try to analyze the feeling as he slid his hands under the elastic, over her satiny belly, to ease her cotton drawers down over her hips. It should've been enough to bring him to his senses.

It wasn't. She smelled of soap, shampoo and something suspiciously like baby powder. She was moving restlessly under his touch, making soft, incoherent demands. "Please—oh, please—" she whimpered.

"Easy, easy, I'll take care of you." He kissed her navel.

She cried out, curling her body around him, and he nearly lost it completely. Slow down, he warned himself. He'd always prided himself on being a considerate lover, and she was obviously inexperienced. "We'll take it slow and easy," he promised.

What he hadn't counted on was Callie. The effect she had on him. He'd never lost control, not since he was fifteen or thereabouts. "Callie, honey—" He kissed his way up the satiny slope of her breast.

"Oh, yes—do that again." Clutching his ears, she held his head so that his mouth covered her rigid nipple. "This is—I'm so embarrassed—oh, oh, oh! I never knew—"

Twisting under him, she sucked in rapid gasps of air, then lifted his head, still holding him by his ears, and kissed his chin, his throat, and finally his nipples. Shyly at first, then with increasing boldness, she used her tongue and her teeth to drive him quietly out of his mind.

Hank let her take the lead, which she did, hungrily, inexpertly, eagerly. Not even when her fingers began fumbling with his belt and zipper did he try to rush her. It nearly killed him. He bore it as long as he could before he stood and quickly shed his jeans and briefs.

And then he knelt between her thighs, every muscle in his body trembling under the strain. "Easy—I'll try not to—"

"Hurry, please hurry up and do it before I explode," she urged, her hands everywhere, fluttering over his shoulders, reaching down to grasp him.

He had to laugh, but it sounded more like crying. She spread her legs wide for him. He could feel her trembling, feel her heat rising to meet him. He met it with his own hard, fierce heat, nudging her open first with his fingers, then with his shaft.

She was ready. He was miles past ready. He felt her legs

wrap around his hips, and he eased himself inside her, hearing her gasp at the same time he felt her tightness knot around him. If the world had come to an end in that moment, he might have been able to stop. As for anything short of that...

"Slow down," he urged in a raspy, barely recognizable whisper. "Let me help you—"

Before he could voice his promise, she began to move. Twitchy, awkward little movements that sent him hurtling into space.

It was a long time before his breathing slowed down enough so that he managed to get out a few words. Not that anything he could say now would help. He tried, anyway. "I'm sorry. God, I'm sorry, Callie."

She was quiet so long he began to feel uneasy. "Callie? Honey, are you still here?"

She sighed. "I told you I didn't know very much about it. Next time I'll probably be better, once I have time to think about it."

His shoulders began to shake. His face was buried in the pillow, but at least he'd had the presence of mind to slide most of his weight off her slight, damp body.

"You don't have to laugh," she said with quiet dignity. "I doubt if you were all that much better the first few times you did it."

"You mean better than I was tonight?"

"I mean better than I was."

Rolling onto his side, he gathered her into his arms. The light was still on—they'd never got around to turning it off—so that he could see her flushed face, the marks of his rough hands, his kisses on her tender skin. Currents of dry, chilled air blew over their damp, overheated bodies, and he pulled the sheet up to cover them. "Honey, have you ever done this before?" He should have been able to tell, but he'd been in too great a rush. She'd been incredibly tight, incredibly sweet, and he'd been incredibly aroused.

"I told you I wasn't exactly an expert."

"Not exactly, hmm?"

He accepted her answer. He would have resented any guy who'd taken her innocence. Wondered whether she'd loved him, whether he'd loved her, and if so, why he hadn't married her and taught her more about the art of good sex.

Callie didn't need any coaching, she was a natural. Once she'd become aroused, he'd never seen such sheer, uninhibited enthusiasm. The trouble was, he'd been burning a short fuse. It had been over much too soon.

"Did you—" He didn't think she had, but then, his own climax had been damn near cataclysmic. The roof could have fallen on his head and he wouldn't have noticed.

Inevitably sanity began to return. Hank didn't particularly welcome it, but then, he'd learned a long time ago that the best way to face a problem was head-on.

Problem number one: he hadn't used protection.

Second problem: he'd just made love to an innocent young woman nearly half his age. A woman who wasn't even his type. One he'd known for less than two weeks. One who worked for him. Any way you looked at it, she was off limits. And the scary thing was that he'd do it all over again.

"If you're asking if I had an orgasm—" Trust Callie, he thought, amused, to put it in technical terms. "I'm not exactly sure. Something happened, though, and it was nice while it lasted. I'm sorry. Maybe next time—"

He groaned. And then he rolled over onto his back, flung one arm over his face, swore a little and began to laugh.

Nice. Right. It had been so nice he was getting hard again just thinking about it.

"Ah, Callie," he murmured, thinking next time—if there

was a next time—he would take it slow and easy, making sure she was with him all the way. But first he'd better lay his cards on the table. "Don't apologize, it was my fault," he confessed. "All I can say in my defense is that I was blindsided. I can't explain it. Even if we'd known each other all our lives, there are too many differences."

He waited. She didn't argue, so he continued. "Age, for one thing. Experience, for another. You're afraid of flying, I was practically born with wings. I don't dance if I can get out of it. I don't watch TV except for world news and a few business programs. I've never even seen this guy Seinfeld. I don't do any of the things your generation does, so you see, I wasn't looking for anything, uh—personal."

He waited for a response, but evidently, he wasn't the only one suffering second thoughts. "Don't say anything right now. Think it over. We've got a decision to make, but it can wait until— Callie? Are you listening?"

A soft snore issued from the still body curled up against him. He swore, chuckled and then swore some more. So much for his good intentions. Maybe they both could do with a little perspective.

Callie woke up sore, puzzled and alone. For several minutes she lay there, wondering why she was naked. Wondering why she was tender in places that had never been tender before.

Wondering if she could possibly have dreamed what she'd dreamed.

Before she even sat up and swung her feet off the bed, she knew it had been no dream. At least not a sleeping dream.

There had been four pillows on the bed. Three of them were on the floor, as was half the covering. There was a shirt dangling half off the chair, and a pair of familiar boots over in the corner.

Hank. Oh, God, had she lost her mind?

A cliché popped into her head. *But I'm not that kind of woman.*

Every woman was that kind of woman with the right man.

And where she was concerned—where far too many women were concerned—Hank Langley was definitely the right man.

She had fallen asleep in his arms after a night of wild, passionate love. Actually it hadn't been a night, it had been more like a few minutes, and it hadn't been love, it had been sex. For both of them. Because they were attracted to each other. They'd both admitted that much, at least. And because she'd just undergone an extremely emotional experience and hadn't been thinking straight, and they were right there between two king-size beds, what was more natural than sex?

"Oh, Lordy. Oh, my mercy, what on earth was I thinking about?"

He was on the phone. Through the open door she could hear his voice, his business voice, sounding unusually terse. Almost as if he were worried. Her first thought was for Manie and she crossed to the door, her feet silent on the thick carpet.

"—to run interference for you. Get Marwick on it right away. Then get Kubecek on the line and tell him I need a list of embassy contacts, pronto."

He was pacing. He was also limping. He looked as if he hadn't slept in weeks, and Callie felt a quick surge of guilt. He was an incredibly important man, not to mention a busy one, for all he tried to seem so laid back when he was at the club. She'd never known a man who carried a portable office with him when he traveled, but then she'd never known a man like Hank Langley.

He punched out, raked a hand through his hair, then punched in another number. "Pete, we'll be taking off at—" Glancing at his watch, he frowned and said, "Better make it fifteen hundred hours. Right. I'll need to be in Washington for an early appointment tomorrow."

There was more. Callie listened because listening was better than thinking, and she wasn't yet ready to think about what had happened, much less what was happening now.

He was leaving. He'd brought her here, done his duty by her and now he was leaving.

Well, fine. Who needed him? She certainly didn't. The house was insured with her father's old agency, and she knew everyone who worked there. By now they probably already had the claims filled out. She could stay with Grace and start making calls—

"Callie? You awake? I ordered us a pot of coffee and some cinnamon rolls. Come have breakfast, we need to talk."

Ten

They were too busy during the next few hours to argue. For reasons she didn't even try to understand, Callie was spoiling for a fight. Hank seemed just as determined to avoid one. He drove her back to look at the remains of her house. She got out and walked around, the harsh morning light revealing in ghastly detail all that was left of the garden and Grandpop's grape arbor. The shed was unharmed, but as it had been on the verge of collapse for decades, it was no great asset. A few of the trees nearest the house would have to come down, but most would probably survive.

"The chimneys will have to go," Hank said. He'd come up behind her so quietly she hadn't even realized he was there.

"They will not! They're not hurting anything." She was reacting emotionally, not rationally. She knew it, but couldn't seem to help herself.

"Callie, they're a hazard. A liability. In legal terms, it's called an attractive nuisance. Half the ads you see on TV today are pitched around mountain climbers. You think any boy could resist a challenge like that?" He gestured to the tall rock tower. "With those handholds, it's a natural for climbing."

"Even little boys are smarter than that."

"Are we talking about the same species here? Me, I'd have been up that sucker like a shot."

She turned away, arms crossed over her bosom. "I don't want to talk about it." She'd dismantle the things herself, rock by rock, brick by brick, before she'd see a child injured there. As for insurance, she had no idea whether or not she had liability. She'd simply continued to pay the premiums on Grandpop's old policy, trusting that her father would have seen that he had adequate coverage. He'd been in the business, for heaven's sake.

"Fine," Hank said calmly, leaving her to wallow in her own miserable doubts.

A cardinal swooped in, hovered for a few moments where the old window feeder had been and then flew away. Oh, Lord, she'd have to do something about the birds. They depended on her, too.

Hank asked, "Who do you need to see besides the insurance agent?"

She sighed. "Grace, I guess. I'd better stop by on the way out and see if I can stay with her for a few days."

He got that steely-eyed look, the one that usually meant he was going to argue with her. "A few days?"

"I'll have to stay here and take care of everything, but first I need to go over my policy and read all the fine print to see what's covered and what isn't. I can't believe I haven't done it before, but—" she sighed. "By then Mama and Daddy will be back."

"What about Manie?"

"What about her?"

"Did I hear you saying something about taking care of her in her old age, or did I just imagine it?"

"I'm doing the best I can, but it takes time, so stop pushing me. Don't you have to be in Washington? I certainly don't need you here." It hung there between them, a matter neither of them was ready yet to address. Ignoring it was like ignoring a fifty-foot neon sign, but Callie managed to do it. Just barely. "In a day or so, once I get everything settled here, I'll go back for Aunt Manie. You can tell her—no, don't tell her anything, I'll call her tonight."

She wandered around the ruins, waving away mosquitoes, pushing with the toe of her sandal at a section of banister, the once-white spindles now charred. Her throat ached from holding back the tears. Grieving was painful enough without having to hold it inside.

Finally driven beyond the limits of her patience, she turned on him and exclaimed, "You're doing this deliberately, aren't you? Stalking me. Trying to get me to hurry up so you can get back to town."

He didn't bat an eye. "I'm only trying to keep you from getting hurt."

"Well, you're too late, I already hurt."

"I meant glass and nails—that kind of thing."

"Oh, I know what you mean—and I appreciate it, I truly do, only…" She swallowed hard, but the painful lump in her throat refused to budge.

"Go ahead and cry. It'll ease some of the pressure. I can hold you if it'll help."

With her whole body still quivering after that last episode? Crying didn't cure anything, it only complicated it. "No, thank you," she said coolly. Then, with her past and future lying in ruins all around her, the acrid stench of it stinging her eyes, she whispered, "Damn, damn, damn," and fell into his arms. Unable to help herself, she cried until there were no tears left. "I'm sorry," she whispered.

"Shh, you're tough as a ten-penny nail. A few tears isn't going to change that." His raspy drawl poured over her like a healing balm.

"I know, but I've ruined your last shirt. Again." She gave a hiccuppy little laugh and pulled away, her throat still aching. Her heart aching. She ached all over, and not just from grieving.

Oh, yes, there was that, too.

Hank crammed a handkerchief into her fist. With one last sniffle, she made a stab at damage control. Then, red-eyed, red-nosed, she took a deep breath, looked him directly in the eye and said, "There. That's over. I promise not to do it again."

"Feel free, anytime. I can always call in help if we need to man the pumps."

She shook her head, but a bit of the sparkle was back in her eyes. "I don't have time to waste, but thanks. If you're ready to go, I've seen enough. More than enough."

Hank drove her to the insurance agency in Yadkinville. He offered to go inside with her, but didn't argue when she refused. "I'd really rather go in alone. I know everyone in the office. They'd all wonder who you are, and I don't want to have to explain you if you don't mind. I've made a list of all I need to find out."

"Take your time, I can make a few calls while I'm waiting."

"What did people like you do before cell phones were invented?"

"People like me? Oh, I don't know…long extension cords?"

That brought—well, not quite a smile, but a few more shadows disappeared from her eyes.

He bought her lunch on the way out of town. By mutual consent, neither of them mentioned what had happened the night before. Hank could wait. First there was the property to be dealt with, and knowing Callie, she would insist on handling things in her own way, in her own time.

It was going to be tricky, but he'd been in tricky situations before. Thrived on 'em, in fact. He just couldn't remember a time when the outcome had been so important.

Back in the car, she asked if she could borrow his phone to call Grace, who hadn't been home when they'd stopped by on the way past. Hank considered telling her he had no intention of leaving her behind. That she was going back to Texas with him in a couple of hours, whether she knew it now or not. Whatever details needed handling, he could handle them for her from his office.

But he knew better than to tip his hand. She had more pride than a two-tailed dog. So he played his ace, instead.

"I've been thinking about Manie. About her future."

Head up. Wary look. "I've already decided what to do. Once I get the insurance money, I'm going to buy us a modular home. Grace loves hers. I can get us a real nice one, one that'll be easy to take care of, because I'll be working again and Aunt Manie doesn't need to be doing heavy housework at her age. Grandpop's house was really too large. I guess the best thing about those old houses is that you could close the door on the parts you aren't using." Her words would have sounded pragmatic if her voice hadn't wavered.

Hank said nothing. He'd learned at an early age that when it came to bargaining, silence was the weapon of choice.

"Well, I still own the property, you know."

"I know. Did you know you've got soot all over your shoes? There's a smudge on the back of your arm, too."

Her shoulders lost some of their military stiffness. She dabbed at her arm, glanced down at her feet and grimaced. "I need a bath."

"We both do."

Their eyes met and then slid apart. Suddenly the focus shifted. Neither of them was ready to deal with it just now, but it couldn't be put off much longer. Sometime over the past twenty-four hours, Hank had come to a conclusion. No matter what Callie thought, Manie was his responsibility. The woman had practically raised him.

Callie was his responsibility because of a momentary weakness on his part. She had never been a part of his original plan. He'd had his future all mapped out. A convenient marriage with a suitable party, followed by a child, or possibly two. No emotional entanglements, at least not with his wife.

Children would be another matter. Something told him he'd make a damned fine daddy once he got the hang of it. At least he knew what *not* to do. If, after a few years, the marriage went sour, he could have counted on the woman to be sensible about it, having covered every possible contingency in a generous prenuptial agreement.

The one contingency he hadn't counted on was Callie.

She was frowning, punching in numbers on his car phone. She wasn't exactly intimidated by technology, but she was still a little wary. After waiting a couple of minutes, she gave up.

"Maybe she's gone to Durham to see her daughter. I'll try again from the hotel."

Wanting to tumble her into his arms and hold her for the

forseeable future, Hank started the engine and backed out of the parking slot.

"Quit frowning," he growled, "you'll get wrinkles."

"What's wrong with wrinkles?"

"Nothing. Laugh lines are better."

She scowled at him. Neither of them spoke again until they turned off onto 421, and then Callie said, "You told Pete fifteen hundred hours. That's three o'clock in the afternoon, isn't it?"

"So?"

"So it's already after two. You're going to have to hurry. You can drop me off at the hotel, grab your things and check out. I'll call Grace again from the lobby. I think I can probably rent a car at the hotel, but if not, I can get a taxi."

"We'll talk about it later."

"You don't have time for later if you're planning on being in Washington tonight. What are you going to do there, anyway?"

She was trying to distract him, bless her little heart. It wasn't going to work, but he had to admit, if anyone could throw him off course, it would be Callie. "Calling on a friend in the diplomatic service, why?"

"Mercy, that sounds important. You don't want to miss your connections."

"I make my own connections, remember?"

"Well—well—oh, just forget it," she snapped.

Good sign. She was going to need all the grit she could muster to get through the next few hours. He intended to push hard. All the same, he kind of liked the soft, damp, clinging Callie.

He began to hum under his breath, and then sang a few words in his rusty baritone, beating time on the steering wheel. The one about Caledonia and her big, hard head?

"Oh, hush up, I've been hearing that wretched song all my life."

"Let me see now, Manie is Romania. Her father was Alaska, her brother, your grandfather, is what? Uwharrie? I think she said he was named after a mountain or something."

"I don't know who started it, but believe me, my daughter, if I ever have one, is going to have a name that can't be turned into a joke."

"You could name her Henry. Hank's not so bad." She made that *tsk* sound that reminded him of Manie, so he told her about his first heartthrob. "I was about thirteen at the time. Old enough to like girls, but not old enough to admit it. Her name was Elizabeth."

"That's a nice, sensible name. Betty. Betsy. Liz."

"We called her Lizard Butt."

"Oh, for goodness' sake!"

But she laughed. First a grin, then a reluctant chuckle. Hank felt as if he'd just pulled off a major deal.

Three o'clock came and went. Evidently Hank had cleared the change with his pilot. He said he'd arranged a late checkout, so Callie took the time to shower while he talked to people in Venezuela and Washington. She wondered if she would ever take such things for granted. Old Doc Teeter used to use an egg timer whenever she had to call long distance from the office.

As soon as they'd got back to the hotel she'd tried Grace again, with the same results. Hank, looking as relaxed as a lizard in the sun, had watched her closely. "It's not a problem, really," she'd assured him. "I can always stay at a motel. I know a real nice one that would be perfect. For that matter, I could stay at my folks' place here in town, only I really need to be closer to Yadkinville."

"Listen, Callie, I've been thinking—"

"Oh, I'd better lock my suitcase. And check the bathroom to see if I forgot anything." She darted away from the scene of the crime, where every single thing reminded her of last night. The big chair where he'd pulled her down onto his lap. The desk he'd bumped when he was carrying her into his bedroom.

His bedroom...

Oh, Lord, she was in way over her head, without so much as an inner tube. Hank wasn't like any man she'd ever dated. Not that there'd been all that many. Certainly none who turned her brain to jelly. None with a mouth she couldn't help watching, wondering what it would taste like—what it would feel like on her lips. On her body.

She took a deep, steadying breath and stepped back into the room that divided their two bedrooms. He was still right where she'd left him, sprawled on the sofa, his booted feet on the coffee table, fingers flying over the keyboard of his laptop computer. It was the one he used for e-mail. He had at least half a dozen computers in his office, more on the plane. Callie had never before met anyone who used different computers for different tasks, but Manie said it had something to do with not putting all his eggs in one basket. Besides, according to her aunt, he owned a company that made those little chip things, so he probably got them at a good price.

While she hovered in the doorway, torn between the need to get on with her business and reluctance to end something so incredibly special, the phone rang. Hank caught it before it could ring again and barked, "Langley. Shoot." He listened, nodded, said, "Passports won't be a problem," and hung up. Callie lifted her suitcase to indicate her readiness to leave, but Hank punched in another number and started talking again, his lazy Texas drawl nowhere in evidence.

She shifted her weight. It wasn't that she was impatient. Well, she was, but only because she had a lot to do. Besides, he'd already given her more time than he could spare. The least she could do was to return the favor.

When she caught him looking at her, she glanced pointedly at her watch. He nodded, but kept right on talking.

Passports. She'd never even owned one. Had never needed one. It was just one of dozens of differences between them. He was cosmopolitan; she was…well, whatever she was, it was not cosmopolitan.

He had a mole on his chest, just below his right collarbone. She knew that much about him. He had gorgeous legs for a man, even with the hair and the scars. There wasn't a single thing about him that wasn't perfect, and that was a problem, too, because she'd learned a long time ago not to waste time dreaming about things she could never have. She'd never gone to Disneyland because they couldn't afford it. She'd never had a horse for the same reason.

Hank probably had a whole flock of horses. He wasn't exactly a cowboy, but he looked as if he'd be every bit as comfortable riding the range as he was dressed in a Western-cut tuxedo at a fancy dress ball. More comfortable, in fact.

Hank was saying, "I've got a couple of contacts at the embassy there, but I can't guarantee their loyalty."

Embassies. She'd never even met anyone who'd been to an embassy, much less someone who knew anyone there. The closest she'd come was when she'd met a congressman's aid when her high school class had made a bus trip to Raleigh to visit the legislature.

"Once the thing goes down, you're going to have to move fast. I can have someone waiting on the other side of the border, but it'll be touch-and-go."

Move fast? Touch-and-go? This didn't sound very much like a standard business call.

"You've got the specs on the Avenger, you know what's required. A cow pasture won't cut it." There was a long pause during which Hank chuckled, swore and shook his head. "Yeah, right. But next time, how about picking a damned desert."

Callie was beginning to think she shouldn't be hearing all this. Whatever was going on, it didn't sound legitimate.

"No, I wouldn't worry the authorities about it. Things are pretty shaky over there, politically. Right. Work out the details, get an idea of the timetable, and I'll check with you when I get in tonight."

He stashed the phone and turned to catch her staring at him. "What?"

"Nothing. I was so busy thinking—um, liability insurance and modular homes and all, I didn't hear a word, not a single word."

"What the devil are you talking about?"

"Nothing. I'm just going over in my mind all the things I have to do over the next few days. If you want to check out now, I'm ready. I can place a few calls from downstairs, and then I'll probably see you back in Texas in a couple of days or so. If you're there. Not that you'll be going anywhere—I mean, there's Washington, but—"

"Callie?"

"What?"

"You're babbling."

"I know. I always do that when I'm nervous."

"Why are you nervous?"

"I'm not. That is, I just have a lot on my mind right now. Things I need to be doing and all. I guess we'd better go on down to the lobby so we can check out on time, hadn't we? I mean, even late checker-outers have to leave sooner or later, and I'd hate for you to get stuck for another night. This place must cost a fortune." *Stupid, stupid, stupid!* He could buy the hotel if he wanted to.

"Sit down, we still have some things to settle."

"Don't you need to be at the airport?"

"I can make it in twenty minutes."

"Not without speeding."

He lifted his eyebrows again, as if to say, "So?"

"Go ahead, risk a ticket if you want to, but I've got to find a place to stay, rent a car, get with the insurance agent and start looking at houses. I want everything under control when I go back for Aunt Manie."

"You still don't get it, do you?"

"Get what?"

"Callie, I'm taking you back to Texas with me. There's not one damned reason for you to stay here. Your folks are gone. You don't have a place to stay or any way to get around. The adjusters can do their job without your personal supervision. As for buying a house—"

"I'm not ordering one from any mail-order catalog, if that's what you're about to say. Listen, we don't have time for this. You've got things to do and I'm sure they're perfectly legal, but I'm so busy I don't even have time to—"

There was one way to shut her up. Not being particularly chivalrous, Hank took it.

When he came up for air, her lips were glistening, her eyes had a dazed look about then and her glasses—God knows where they were. They were no longer on her face.

They were both breathing hard. "Why on earth did you do that?" she gasped.

"Seemed like a pretty good idea to me."

"Yes, well—it wasn't, it only confuses the issue and—"

"Wastes time?"

"That's not what I was about to say."

"What were you about to say, Caledonia?"

"How do I know? You can't expect me to remember everything when you—when you do—things like that."

"Things like kissing you?"

She blushed. He watched, fascinated, while the hot, sweet color rose up her throat to stain her cheeks. "Look at me, Callie." She deliberately avoided his eyes. For a woman who made a virtue of being direct, it was a dead giveaway. "Tell me you didn't want it."

"There's a time and a place for everything, and this is neither."

He gave her full marks for effort. "Yeah, well—you're right about the time, but what's wrong with the place?"

Her eyes cut directly to the bedroom door, open to reveal part of a king-size bed that had been freshly made.

It could easily be unmade. He said as much, and she shoved him away and raked trembling fingers through her hair.

"You think Manie would object?" His words were teasing. His eyes were not. "You're probably right. She'd skin us both alive. So what if I promise to make an honest woman of you, do you think that would satisfy her?"

"I don't know what you're talking about."

He considered it a moment. "I think you do. I think you had a pretty good idea last night where this thing between us was headed." She looked so stricken he almost relented, but as long as he'd come this far, he might as well go all the way. "Marry me, Callie."

Her jaw dropped. She blinked up at him. "Excuse me?"

"Excuse me is not an acceptable answer."

From an early age, Hank had been blessed with charisma. With the kind of charm that could lure birds out of trees and women into his bed.

Now, nearing the age of forty, it had been honed down

until any hint of youthful charm was gone. Worn away by time and experience. The charisma was still there, but it was mostly in the eyes, a tool he seldom used to get what he wanted.

He used it now. He wanted Callie.

"Callie? I've got a proposition for you. If you want the spreadsheet version, I can do that, too. The pros and cons, pluses and minuses. Better yet, I can have you back with Manie by suppertime, and you can talk it over with her. I promise you this—if you still want to, and if Manie agrees to move back here, I'll fly you both back so you can pick out your house together. Do we have a deal?"

Eleven

They had a deal. A shaky, provisional deal, but under the circumstances, Callie was in no condition to resist. She had one major factor working against her: she was in love with the guy. Not infatuated. She wasn't terribly experienced, but over the years she'd learned the difference between love and infatuation. She'd had what Grandpop called crushes on several boys, but not one of them would she ever have considered marrying.

"Got that look about you, gal," he used to say. "Don't do nothin' foolish, y'hear?"

And, of course, with her own parents as an example, she never had. Or almost never. Until now.

"It don't hurt a man to have a few flaws. God didn't make no perfect ones, but when it comes to settlin' in for the long haul, be sure the two of you have respect for one another. It'll still be there when you're too old to do more'n set on the front porch and hold hands."

After careful consideration—because she was, after all, known for her common sense—Callie decided that more than any man she'd ever known, she respected Hank Langley for his strength, his integrity and his kindness. Grandpop would have approved of him.

But it wasn't respect that made her knees go weak or her heart flutter like a caged wild bird. It wasn't respect that made her want to tear off his clothes and have her way with him until neither one of them had the strength to fall out of bed.

And if that wasn't enough to short out every brain cell she possessed, she didn't know what was.

"You're mighty quiet," Hank observed as he seated her in the car that had been waiting at the private airport just outside Royal. "I'm still waiting for an answer."

Callie cleared her throat and tried to look stern. "I said I'd think about it. I'm still thinking." Emotionally exhausted, she'd slept during the entire flight back to Texas.

"And?"

"And I'm not finished thinking about it yet, but if I decide to do it, it doesn't mean I'm going to roll over and play dead," she warned him. "I'm too independent for that, so if you're looking for a doormat, I'm not the wife you want."

"Duly noted."

It didn't help her claim of independence that she'd come back to Texas with him, leaving her business back home unfinished. Her whole life was unraveling faster than she could snatch up the loose ends and weave them back into place.

She almost wished he hadn't asked her to marry him. If he had any idea how much she wanted to grab the steering wheel, pull the car off onto the shoulder, slam on the brakes and kiss the living daylights out of him, she wouldn't even stand a chance.

Was it a simple case of lust? Biology? Chemistry? Whatever it took to spark an explosion between two people? Was it honestly, truly love, or just a strong case of mutual attraction added to liking and respect? How was a woman supposed to know?

She sighed. Whatever it was, it hadn't come with a list of ingredients, nor even a warning sign.

By the time they reached the club, there were only half a dozen or so vehicles left in the parking lot, most belonging to staff. A light came on over the garage where Hank kept his cars, his pickup truck and his motorcycle. A moment later, his driver appeared in the doorway. Hank waved him away.

"It's late. I need to go home," Callie murmured.

"You are home."

Hank switched off the engine and sat there, face forward, hands still on the steering wheel. The upper part of his body was in shadow, so Callie allowed her gaze to stray to his muscular thighs.

Big mistake. She swallowed hard, took a deep breath and tried again. "I didn't mean back home in Yadkin County, I meant home to Aunt Manie's house."

"I didn't mean home in Royal, I meant home with me. I thought we'd settled it. Honey, your home is with me, whether we're in Texas, North Carolina or halfway to the moon."

He turned to her just as light from a passing car delineated his bronzed, masculine features, making him look for a moment like some ancient warrior from another age.

Had a man like that actually asked her to marry him, or had she only imagined it? She hadn't imagined what had happened in that king-size bed last night. At its wildest, her imagination wasn't up to a task of such magnitude.

"Hungry?"

"What? Oh. No, thanks, I couldn't eat a bite."

"Still queasy?"

"I'm fine, but—Hank, we've got to get something straight."

"Yeah, we have. Come on upstairs and we'll sort out the logistics."

Panic was beginning to set in. Callie told herself it was only jet lag—that and the fact that her life seemed to have been swept up in an avalanche these past few days. First a fancy ball, for heaven's sake, then her house burning down, and then flitting across the country in a jet plane as if it were no more than driving down to the local IGA.

Now an oil millionaire claimed he wanted to marry her. What was she supposed to do? Even though he didn't feel like a millionaire; even though he was just Hank, and she wanted him more than she'd ever wanted anything in her entire life, it would never work, not in a million years. He was rich and sophisticated. She was poor and country. She was plain; he was fancy. He had a passport and a flock of platinum credit cards, and all she had was a high school diploma, a social security card, and a perfect attendance certificate from Sunday School.

"I called ahead and ordered us some supper."

"I'm not hungry." And that was another thing. He was used to having whatever he wanted, when he wanted it. She'd always had to plan ahead, work and save, and then weigh genuine needs against frivolous desires.

Like a lamb to the slaughter, Callie let him lead her upstairs. Passing close to the kitchen, they heard the sound of soft laughter and clinking dishes. Someone was playing a radio, and it reminded her of the way her mother always tuned into WTQR and danced around the kitchen to Brooks and Dunn, or harmonized with Reba.

She was simply homesick. And no gentlemen's club in the middle of the Wild West could ever take the place of her real home.

But then she reminded herself that her parents' loft had never been her home, the apartment they'd lived in when she was growing up was now a strip mall and Grandpop's house lay in ruins.

When her face threatened to crumple from exhaustion and sheer discouragement, she bit her lip and scowled.

Hank let them in, collecting a stack of mail as they passed Manie's desk. "Why not have a nice hot soak while I see what Mouse left for us in the refrigerator? I'll set your bag in the dressing room, but feel free to borrow anything of mine."

As if she would dare. Even wearing the hotel's bathrobe, she'd half expected the manager to rush in and accuse her of appropriating hotel property. Which just went to show how totally unsuited she was to be the wife of a man like Hank Langley.

"After that, we'll get down to brass tacks."

She stared at him mutely for a moment, and then turned and opened the first door she came to, which turned out to contain banks of computers and other esoteric equipment. With a stricken look, she backed out, and Hank took pity on her.

"Honey, calm down, nobody's going to hurt you. You haven't been kidnapped, nobody's holding you against your will, which reminds me..."

Which reminded him that he'd better check in with Greg ASAP. The mission was slated to go in stages, and the first stage should be ready to launch in approximately thirty-six hours to rescue the Princess and her son.

That left him barely enough time to settle things with Callie and ram the necessary paperwork through.

"Well, where the devil is your blooming bathroom, anyway?" she blurted. "Out in the backyard?"

She looked mad as a yellow jacket, but Hank knew it was mostly exhaustion. That and confusion. "Next door on the right," he told her. Very few people had ever been invited into his private domain. Of those few, only two were female. The housekeeper and Manie, who had never stood on ceremony where any of the Langleys were concerned.

She glared at him, as if not trusting him to steer her right. A tired smile creased his face. Whether or not she was ready to admit it, she wanted him as much as he wanted her. A man could usually sense these things. When it came to hiding her feelings, Callie was no match for him. "You've got twenty minutes," he warned her gently. "After that, I'll expect an answer to my proposal."

"Hank, I told you—"

"I said an answer, not an argument. A simple affirmative will suffice."

"It wasn't a simple proposal." She escaped with the last word, which was probably just as well. Needing food, a drink, a bath and a good night's sleep, he let himself into the communications room. To say it was state-of-the-art would be an understatement. With a variety of sophisticated equipment, some of which was still in the experimental stage, he had instant access to every country in the civilized world, and a few that were still pretty borderline.

He punched in a number, waited for a click that signaled the encryption system was working, and said, "Langley here. Look, you're all set up on the other end, but there might be a few dicey spots. You're going to have to go in at night—yeah, I've got that covered, but— Right. No problem. The money will be waiting, but cover your tracks, man. My contacts say this Ivan character has more tentacles than a tankful of centipedes.''

After he rang off, Hank sat and stared unseeingly at the giant map that was dotted with pushpins. Then, checking the time, he rose stiffly, stretched and went in search of his lady.

Looking scrubbed, sleepy and even more belligerent, she was wearing his navy-brocaded bathrobe. He'd known, of course, that she didn't have one of her own, at least not with her. It occurred to him that everything she owned except for the few things she'd brought west with her had probably been lost in the fire.

Priority one: outfit her from the skin out, the way he'd been wanting to do ever since he'd seen her that first day in those limp cottons.

Correction: priority one was getting her to agree to marry him, right now, no waiting, no engagement, no legal hassles.

''Feel better?'' he drawled.

''Not especially.''

''You need food. Want to dine first, or settle this business about my propopsal? I believe you said it wasn't a simple proposal. Care to elaborate on that?''

''Not really, I'm hungry.''

''Humor me while I set out our supper.'' He led the way to a formal dining room he almost never used. ''Tea, coffee or milk?''

''Milk, please, and don't try to confuse me. We both know I'm no expert on marriage proposals.''

''What, you want the hearts and flowers version? I could go down on bended knee, but it would hurt like hell and I'm a bear when I'm in pain.''

''You're a bear even when you're not in pain. Hank, if

this is your conscience speaking, forget it. I'm old enough to know what I'm doing. What happened—well, it was a—a mutual thing.''

"I seriously doubt that,'' he said ruefully with just the shadow of a smile.

"Well, if it's pity you're offering, I don't need that, either. I got sort of emotional for a little while, but I'm fine now, honestly. In fact, you were right. Talking things over with Aunt Manie in person is the smart thing to do, because she's involved, too.''

He swore softly. Callie said, "I don't know why you're so upset, I'm letting you off the hook. This is practically the twenty-first century, after all, and we're both—I think the term is single, consenting adults.'' The look he sent her didn't bear interpretation. "Besides, you've already done so much, I'll never be able to repay you. You don't have to take it to extremes.''

"Dammit all to hell, Callie, what kind of fool do you take me for?''

"I don't know—a sweet one? A generous one? One who's determined not to let me take Aunt Manie back home with me? Which means, I guess, you're a selfish one, too, but that's all right. I know you're fond of her, but that doesn't mean you have to take on the care and feeding of all her relatives. Aside from Daddy, I'm her only blood kin, which makes me the logical one to look after her in her declining years, and I really want to do it. I like having family around me. It gives me a sense of purpose.''

He muttered something under his breath. She put it down to the fact that he was probably as tired and hungry and stressed as she was.

"Women are just naturally better at that sort of thing than men, so don't you see? It's the best solution all around. You can come to visit anytime you're in the neighborhood, you'll always be—'' Breaking off, she tilted her head to stare at him. "What? Why are you staring at me that way?"

He slapped two plates down on the table and said, "Wait here. I want to show you something." And then he disappeared into the next room.

Callie half rose, then sat back down. Phrases like "up the creek without a paddle," and "in over her head" came to mind.

A minute later Hank returned and handed her a framed photograph. It was a grainy black-and-white snapshot that had obviously been enlarged. She looked at him, and then studied the picture of a young woman dressed in clothes reminiscent of the forties, or maybe the fifties. She was wearing a catcher's mitt and laughing at a little boy with spiky hair and a snaggletoothed grin who was clutching a baseball bat almost as long as he was.

"Who—?" And then she recognized the woman. Not the child, but something about the woman reminded her of her own father. The nose, the forehead... "Oh, my mercy, it's Aunt Manie, isn't it? But who's the little boy?"

When there was no response, she peered closer. Harsh shadows disguised the child's features, but nothing could disguise the childish arrogance of his stance. As if he were Babe Ruth and Mark McGwire all rolled into one. "It's you, isn't it?" she whispered.

"She's the only mother I've ever really known. I love her, Callie, but that has nothing to do with why I asked you to marry me."

For a long time, neither of them said a word. And then Callie whispered, "Damn these Texas rules. I never even had a prayer, did I?"

"That applies to both of us."

"I've heard of marrying for the sake of a child, but this

is crazy. Nobody marries for the sake of a sixty-nine-year-old woman.''

''Seventy-two, but don't let on I told you.''

She'd lost her appetite. Carefully she set the photograph aside. With her heavy sterling fork, she rearranged the chicken salad and poached pears Mouse had prepared to go with the tiny cloverleaf rolls. Sighing, she said, ''Then why? Why did you ask me to marry you, and don't try to tell me it was because I—because we—''

''Slept together?''

''Whatever you want to call it.''

''At this point, I'm as out of my depth as you are. You want my take on it?''

''Please.''

''All right, I admit that lately I've been thinking of something along the lines of a marriage of convenience, at least until we got to know each other better. The trouble is, celibacy's not going to work here, not after last night.''

''Lust is not a sound basis for marriage.''

''Tell me about it,'' he said bitterly. ''I went that route once before. It was a dead end. What I had in mind this time around was a sensible, mutually beneficial arrangement with all the rules clearly spelled out beforehand and agreed to by both sides. You get a home, I don't have to worry about choosing between Pansy and Bianca, and—''

''And Aunt Manie will be taken care of.''

''Yeah, well…we'll talk about that later. Right now, we have to come to some agreement. It would help if you'd say yes.''

Wearing his bathrobe, the one that hung behind the bathroom door, she looked young and tired and confused. He wanted to take pity on her and send her to bed, but dammit, not when he was this close to his goal.

''I still don't understand why it has to be marriage.''

"You want me to spell it out? All right, here goes. Your first offense was trampling all over every damned privacy fence I'd erected. Privacy is important to a man in my position."

"I did that? I didn't mean to," she whispered.

"You asked. I'm telling you. Do me the courtesy of not interrupting, because I don't like admitting my weaknesses. Okay, so you showed up and I started acting like a randy kid his first time out of the barn. I'm not saying you did it deliberately, any more than I deliberately set it up. I will admit I took advantage of the circumstances."

She stared at him mutely. Next thing he knew, she'd probably be snoring. "I'll even admit I lost control. I didn't use protection. Hell, I didn't even take the time to see to your satisfaction first. For a man with some twenty-five years of experience, who enjoys a certain reputation as a skilled lover, that's a flat-out disgrace. Any other woman would have raised hell, but not you."

She was awake. From the neck up, she turned red as a pepper, but she stared him square in the eyes. "Callie, honey, don't you see? What you've gone and done is, you've messed up my mind at a time when I can't afford the luxury of a distraction."

"The Alpha thing?"

"What do you know about Alpha?"

Her high color left as swiftly as it had arisen. "Only that you and Greg Hunt and that nice Mr. Churchill are involved in something that needs passports and embassies and that's probably why you need to be in Washington instead of sitting here arguing with me."

"So how about cutting me some slack? Marry me?"

"Because of Alpha?"

They had given up any pretense of eating. The elegant feast served on bone china, imported wine and cold milk served in antique crystal—all of it could have been sawdust served on paper plates.

"Not because of Alpha," he said quietly. Rising, he held out his hand. Like a sleepwalker, Callie placed her hand in his and allowed him to lead her from the room. Neither of them pretended they didn't know what was happening.

And this time, Hank promised himself, it would be different. This time was for Callie. Before he even thought about taking his own pleasure he was going to make her bones melt, make her whimper, make her shout out his name. And then repeat the performance again and again, as long as his middle-aged body could hold up.

Briefly he thought about spinning her a line. It wouldn't be the first time he'd lured a woman into his bed with a bit of silver-tongued patter, although usually he didn't have to bother.

Lately he hadn't even been tempted.

At his bedroom door, she said, "We're going to do it again, aren't we?"

He choked on a laugh. "God, I sincerely hope so."

"Well, all right, but that doesn't mean I have to marry you."

"The offer's still open, regardless."

She shot him a suspicious look. His bedroom was done in desert shades, with few softening touches. Except for the custom-built bed, she didn't even give it a glance.

"Take all the time you need. Tomorrow you can move your things in here, and in a day or so we can start looking around for a house. I figure the club's no place to raise a family."

"Didn't you hear what I just said? If we're going to talk about marriage, I have a right to present my side, too."

"Callie?" He turned her to face him, cupped her chin

between thumb and forefinger and lifted her face to his. "Hush up, sweetheart. It'll all work out, trust me."

"I just thought you might want to know that I gave it more thought while I was in the bathtub."

His mouth hovered over hers. "Hmm?"

"You told me to think about it, so I did."

"Callie, not now. I'm getting ready to make love to you, and this time—"

"I know, and I want you to, honestly I do. I like it. But remind me to tell you when we're finished about the seven reasons why I'll probably marry you, and the two reasons why I might not."

Turning away, he raked his fingers through his hair. "I'm out of my mind. No sane man would marry a woman who can turn him on and tie his mind in knots at the same time."

She smelled of his bath soap. He wondered what, if anything, she was wearing underneath his silk brocaded bathrobe. He couldn't figure out if she was sly as a fox or innocent as a day-old chick.

He did know she was too damn young for him, but he told himself that for a woman who'd spent her entire twenty-two years in a town about half the size of Royal, she had more on the ball than any of the women he knew who'd spent a lifetime, not to mention a fortune, soaking up what passed for culture on several continents.

"You're frowning. Does your head hurt?" she asked.

"No. Yeah, oh, hell, sweetheart, come here."

He swept her up and carried her to his bed, not even bothering to fold back the spread. He was in no condition to think, much less to argue. That could come later. Sometime during the next fifty years he might even come up with a few answers.

This time there was no hesitation. In no more time than

it took for her to untie the sash of his robe, Hank shed his shirt and shucked out of his jeans and briefs in one motion, stumbling only when he tried to pull them off over his boots.

Her laughter was nearly his undoing. "Well, I could have told you that," she said. "Shoes first, then britches. Oh, my, you're gorgeous. I love looking at you."

"You're a witch." He came down beside her and scooped her into his arms.

"The wicked witch of the west?"

"East, west, whatever—just remember, you're *my* witch."

"I'll have to practice."

"Feel free." Flopping over onto his back, Hank spread his arms and tried to wipe the grin off his face. Playfulness in bed was new to him. He had a lot to learn.

"I mean about making love. I'm not the romantic type, you probably noticed that."

"Right. It's one of the first things I noticed about you. You don't get your knickers in a wad if a man doesn't spend all his time paying homage to your beauty."

"You'd hardly do that. But then, you knew what I looked like when you asked me to marry you, so it's not like you're buying a pig in a poke."

"Honey, we've got a lot to learn about each other, but now's not the time." She was wearing another pair of plain white cotton drawers. How could something so clean and wholesome turn him on the way she did? God help him if he ever saw her in skimpy, bias-cut peach-colored silk, his own particular weakness.

He'd promised himself he'd take his time, only he hadn't known a single touch, the mere sight of her lying in his bed, could ignite such a frenzy of white-hot sexual need.

"Hush now," he growled. Rolling over her, he began to

explore her mouth while her hands fluttered over his shoulders, down his back to his buttocks. She stroked and patted him there. Feelings swelled inside him, feelings that were too new, too scary, too powerful to put into words. The best he could do was put his whole heart into kissing her. Which he did. Thoroughly, fiercely, hungrily. That's when he discovered that his heart was no longer his own, he'd already given it away.

Her fingers kneaded his flesh, and when his mouth dragged down her throat to her breast and he began to suckle her nipples, she twisted frantically beneath him.

"Hank, I can't bear to wait much longer," she gasped.

"It'll be worth it, I promise. This time is for you."

But it was for both of them. That time, and the next time. If he hadn't been half-dead from a lack of sleep over the past few nights, there would have been a third time as well.

"I never knew—" she whispered. "I never dreamed— I can't believe…"

"Believe," he told her, his voice as unsteady as his hands. He felt around for various articles of clothing, untangled and sorted them out. "Or don't believe. I've got nothing better to do for the next twenty or thirty years than teaching you what lo—what sex is all about."

"I dare you to say it."

"What, sex?"

"You were going to say love. Don't, if it bothers you. It was one of the things on my list—one of the reasons for marrying you, but it can wait."

"Are you sure?" He wasn't comfortable talking about his emotions, but if she wanted it in writing, signed, sealed and notarized, she could have it. Because he did. It had hit him with the force of a sledgehammer, scaring him damned near spitless.

He was wiped out. She seemed almost energized. He

could see right now he was going to have to stock up on vitamins.

"Well, I just thought you might want to know. I love you," she said calmly, "and there's also the fact that I might be carrying your baby."

He just about swallowed his Adam's apple.

"Chances are pretty slim," she went on, "but you can never be absolutely sure about these things. It takes a few weeks for—"

"Whoa. Back up and run that by me again. You're marrying me because you might be pregnant?" He should have been cheering. Hell, that was what he'd been angling for, wasn't it? A quiet, trouble-free wife who would bear him a son and heir?

But that was before he'd met Callie.

"That was number one on my list, but it's not the only reason. Aunt Manie told me about this house your parents lived in, and—"

"My father and his fourth wife, not my parents."

"Yes, well…the club's real nice, but I can't see living there with Manie and our children."

He wanted to yell, "Slow down!" He wanted to wake up the judge and marry Callie before she came to her senses.

Even more than that, he wanted to catch his breath, roll over and spend the forseeable future convincing her that she wasn't making a mistake.

In other words, he was a basket case.

"Happens I own a small ranch out in the country. About forty-five sections, a house, the usual outbuildings. We could look it over in the next few days, see if you think it can be brought up to standard."

"Does anything grow there?"

"You mean other than mesquite, mulberry and china-berry trees?"

The fingers of his left hand touched the fingers of her right hand, tangled and held. "Yes, well...you know Aunt Manie likes to grow things. It's awfully dry once you get away from Royal. Do you suppose we could irrigate?"

I can't believe I'm lying in bed with a woman, having a conversation about irrigating a damned defunct ranch.

He traced a heart in the palm of her hand, heard her catch her breath and smiled. "Make an appointment with your boss to look over all properties."

"Done. Is this a good time to talk about prenuptial agreements? I overheard Pansy talking to Bianca in the ladies' room at the ball about who's the best lawyer and what to go for. I don't think they were talking about anyone in particular, just husbands and agreements in general."

His head came up off the pillow, and he rolled over to stare at her. "I know, I know," she said hurriedly, "I shouldn't have been listening, but I was feeling sort of— you know. The champagne and all—and, well, anyway, I thought the simplest thing to do was wait until they left to come out of the—the booth."

Hank didn't know whether to laugh, swear, or give up. At least they seemed to have settled one thing: she was going to marry him. "You can have one if you want one, but I'm not insisting." He'd fire every lawyer on his payroll if they tried to force the issue.

"I do. I want it in writing that Aunt Manie can live with us, and that you'll take care of her—" He tried to interrupt, but she kept right on talking. "And that you'll be a full-time father to any children we might have, and that you'll let me have as many as I want. Children, that is. And that you won't yell at me when they're around, because it would make them feel awful, and I'd never want a child of mine to go through that.'' She took a deep breath, clutching his hand, but still staring up at the overhead.

He waited. ''Is that it?''

She swallowed audibly and said, ''All the important stuff, anyway.''

''I've got a condition of my own.''

Warily she turned her head to look at him. ''I guess I'd better hear it now, before this discussion goes any further.''

''I love you. I can't think of anything else it could possibly be. In case it matters, I've had all my shots, I like kids and animals, I don't have any bad habits—well, none I can't handle—and—'' He broke off and looked at her apologetically. ''I guess that about sums it up.''

''I guess it does,'' she said softly, and came into his arms as if she'd finally made her way home.

Epilogue

Wearing a plain ivory silk dress and looking as composed as any woman with a suspicious glow on her face could possibly look under the circumstances, Callie buried her face in the bouquet of orchids and stephanotis.

Mercy, she hadn't even had time to catch her breath.

Hank was openly gloating. Wearing a yellow rosebud in his lapel, he looked devastatingly handsome. His best man, Sterling Churchill, kept glancing at his watch. Callie happened to know he had a plane to catch. Something to do with this mysterious Alpha thing, which was the main reason why she'd let herself be bulldozed into marrying with such indecent haste.

Her parents couldn't make it, which hurt more than she'd thought it would, but between them, Aunt Manie and Susan Wilkins, her bridesmaid and new best friend, had more than made up the loss. Aunt Manie had brought along her fiancé, Marion Jones, greenhouse tycoon, grower of fine orchids and half owner of a baseball team. Callie had never even known her aunt was a baseball fan.

"Ready? Here, take this handkerchief, every woman in my family for generations has carried it for her wedding. I doubt that I'll ever get to use it." Susan Wilkins poked the lacy scrap in her hand, adjusted her headdress and signaled to the musicians.

Just as the trumpet, two fiddles, three guitars and a banjo struck up the first notes of the wedding march, the sound of a jet plane could be heard overhead.

Sterling glanced at his watch again, caught Hank's eyes and nodded.

Susan walked slowly toward where the minister waited in front of the massive fireplace, her gaze never once straying to the handsome, gray-eyed man standing proudly beside the groom.

"My friends, fellow Texans and the few Tarheels who are gathered here today on this joyous occasion," the minister intoned.

Callie bit her lip, eyes glistening with tears of happiness.

Hank leaned over and whispered, "No bawling on our wedding day, Caledonia. Texas rules, remember?" She laughed out loud, and then so did he.

As the venerable old club rang with the sound of music, cheers and laughter, the bridesmaid glanced over at the best man and shook her head. Long after the preacher had pronounced the couple man and wife, an odd gleam seemed to linger in the eyes of the tall young business tycoon.

* * * * *

Watch for the next installment of the
Texas Cattleman's Club *where the romance between*
Susan Wilkins and Sterling Churchill causes sparks to
fly, and more of the ultra-secret Alpha mission is
uncovered in CINDERELLA'S TYCOON
by Caroline Cross
Coming to you from Silhouette Desire
in September 1999.
And now for a sneak preview of
CINDERELLA'S TYCOON, *please turn the page.*

The telephone was ringing.

Head down, arms braced against the slick white shower tile, Sterling Churchill tensed at the shrill sound, the muscles in his back tightening reflexively beneath the pounding spray.

Why the hell doesn't Maxine get that? he wondered irritably a second before he remembered he was alone in the house. His return from Obersbourg earlier than planned had sent his housekeeper rushing off to the grocery store.

As it was, Sterling was just glad to be home in one piece, the mission successfully completed. To the relief of everyone involved, Princess Anna and young William were now safely in Royal, Texas.

He yawned. While the first part of the rescue had mostly involved a lot of time-consuming research and planning, once they'd put their plan into motion, things had happened fast. As a consequence, for the past week he'd operated on too little sleep and too much adrenaline, and it was finally taking its toll.

Not that he was complaining. Lately, his life had seemed increasingly empty, and he'd welcomed the break in his routine. And he had to admit that, despite the potential danger, he'd enjoyed the adrenaline rush of eluding the Obersbourg Palace Guard as their small group—he, Greg Hunt and Forrest Cunningham, the Princess and her little boy—made their way to the small, private airfield where their plane had been waiting.

The phone continued to ring.

Abruptly out of patience, Sterling straightened, turned off the water and shoved open the door. Snatching a burgundy bath sheet off the heated rack, he wrapped it around his waist and stormed into his oversize bedroom, stopping before the inlaid table next to the bed. He snatched up the receiver. *"What?"*

"Hello? Mr. Churchill?"

"Who's this?"

"It's Mike Tarlick. Margaret's son?"

Some of his tension drained away. Margaret Tarlick had worked as a secretary in Sterling's main office of Churchill Enterprises.

"What can I do for you, Mike?"

"Actually, it's what I can do for you, Mr. Churchill. I'm working as a tech at the Buddy Clinic these days, and I overheard something I think you ought to know."

Sterling scowled, his mood instantly deteriorating. The Buddy Clinic was local lingo for the Buddy Williams's Clinic for Reproductive Technology. Ever since Sterling's marriage had gone bust, he'd done his level best to put the fertility clinic's existence out of his mind, associating it as he did with his most bitter personal failure.

"You understand, I could lose my job if the Clinic ever

finds out I called you," Mike went on, his voice growing anxious. "But I just thought...after all you've done for Mom...this is something you have a right to know."

Sterling seriously doubted there was anything Margaret's son could tell him that he didn't already know. He and Teresa had undergone every test known to mankind, and the Clinic still had been unable to come up with a reason why they couldn't conceive. Nevertheless... "You've got my word that I won't tell anyone I talked to you."

Mike took a deep breath. "Okay. I overheard two of the nurses talking. It seems there was a mix-up. A patient came in to be artificially inseminated and somehow the lab misread the code on the storage vial. The donor specimen that was used was...yours."

"What?" Sterling's head snapped up, his exhaustion suddenly forgotten.

"I don't know what happened, Mr. Churchill, honest. Everyone here is always so careful. I wouldn't have bothered you, except that I pulled the chart and the test came back positive and I thought you ought to know."

Sterling forced himself to concentrate as he tried to sort through the avalanche of information. Finally, he said carefully. "What test came back positive?"

"The pregnancy test," the young man said matter-of-factly.

For a second Sterling couldn't seem to breathe. "The woman is *pregnant?*"

"Yeah. That's why I thought you ought to know."

Damn. Damn it all to hell. Some stranger was going to have *his* baby? "What's this pregnant woman's name, Mike?"

"Oh, I don't think..."

Sterling squeezed his eyes shut. "Please. I'd consider it a personal favor."

There was silence, and then Mike Tarlick said with obvious reluctance, "I really shouldn't do this, but I guess... I mean, I suppose you have the right to know. It's Wilkins. Susan Wilkins."

The name seemed vaguely familiar. Sterling struggled to put a face with it. For a moment nothing surfaced, and then it came to him. Susan Wilkins was that nondescript little redhead who worked at the library, the one who was a friend of Callie Langley's.

"Mr. Churchill? Are you there?"

"Yeah. Yeah, of course I am. I appreciate the call, Mike. I won't forget it. Thanks."

"You're wel—"

Sterling dropped the receiver into the cradle, uncaring that he'd cut the young man off. Ripping the towel free of his waist, he strode toward the huge walk-in closet, his mind whirling.

Like it or not, sleep would have to wait. Not only did he have a call to make at the fertility clinic, but—more importantly—he had urgent business with a certain red-headed librarian.

SILHOUETTE® Desire®

MAN of the MONTH

May '99
LOVE ME TRUE
#1213 by ANN MAJOR

June '99
THE STARDUST COWBOY
#1219 by Anne McAllister

July '99
PRINCE CHARMING'S CHILD
#1225 by Jennifer Greene

August '99
THAT BOSS OF MINE
#1231 by Elizabeth Bevarly

September '99
LEAN, MEAN & LONESOME
#1237 by Annette Broadrick

October '99
FOREVER FLINT
#1243 by Barbara Boswell

MAN OF THE MONTH

For ten years Silhouette Desire
has been giving readers the ultimate in sexy,
irresistible heroes. Come join the celebration as some
of your favorite authors help celebrate our
anniversary with the most sensual, emotional love
stories ever!

Available at your favorite retail outlet.

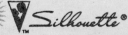

SILHOUETTE®

Desire

A hidden passion, a hidden child,
a hidden fortune.

Revel in the unfolding of these
powerful, passionate...

SECRETS!

A brand-new miniseries from
Silhouette Desire® author

Barbara McCauley

July 1999
BLACKHAWK'S SWEET REVENGE (SD #1230)
Lucas Blackhawk wanted revenge! And by marrying
Julianna Hadley, he would finally have it. Was exacting
revenge worth losing this new but true love?

August 1999
SECRET BABY SANTOS (SD #1236)
She had never meant to withhold the truth from Nick Santos,
but when Maggie Smith found herself alone and pregnant, she
had been unable to face the father of her child. Now Nick was
back—and determined to discover what secrets Maggie was
keeping....

September 1999
KILLIAN'S PASSION (SD #1242)
Killian Shawnessey had been on his own since childhood.
So when Cara Sinclair showed up in his life claiming he had
a family—and had inherited millions—Killian vowed to keep
his loner status. Would Cara be able to convince Killian that
his empty future could be filled by a shared love?

Secrets! available at your favorite retail outlet store.

Silhouette®

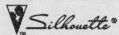

Coming this September 1999
from SILHOUETTE BOOKS
and bestselling author

RACHEL LEE

CONARD
COUNTY:
Boots & Badges

Alicia Dreyfus—a desperate woman on the run—
is about to discover that she *can* come home
again…to Conard County. Along the way she
meets the man of her dreams—and brings together
three other couples, whose love blossoms beneath
the bold Wyoming sky.

Enjoy four complete, **brand-new** stories in one
extraordinary volume.

Available at your favorite retail outlet.